THE AUTHOR

SHEILA WATSON was born in New Westminster, British Columbia, in 1909. She took her B.A. (1931) and M.A. (1933) from the University of British Columbia, and then taught in elementary and high schools on the B.C. mainland and on Vancouver Island before beginning further graduate studies in English literature at the University of Toronto after the Second World War.

In the early 1950s, Watson lived in Calgary, where she wrote much of her novel *The Double Hook*. In the same decade, she continued her graduate studies, working on Wyndham Lewis under the supervision of Marshall McLuhan.

In 1961 Watson joined the Department of English at the University of Alberta. With colleagues there, she was a founder and editor of *White Pelican*, an avant-garde journal of literature and the visual arts. She retired from teaching in 1975, and moved to Nanaimo, British Columbia.

In 1992 she published *Deep Hollow Creek*, a novel she had written in the late 1930s.

Sheila Watson died in Nanaimo, British Columbia, in 1998.

DEEP HOLLOW CREEK

SHEILA WATSON

AFTERWORD BY
JANE URQUHART

The following note appeared in the original edition: The author wishes to express her thanks to F.T. Flahiff and Ellen Seligman.

Copyright © 1992 Estate of Sheila Watson
Afterword copyright © 1999 by Jane Urquhart

First published in 1992 by McClelland & Stewart

First New Canadian Library edition 1999
This New Canadian Library edition 2010

Library and Archives Canada Cataloguing in Publication

Watson, Sheila, 1909-1998
    Deep Hollow Creek / Sheila Watson ; afterword by Jane Urquhart.

(New Canadian library)
ISBN 978-0-7710-9458-3

    I. Title. II. Series: New Canadian library

PS8545.A88D4 2010   C813'.54   C2010-900038-2

We acknowledge the financial support of the Government of Canada through the Book Publishing Industry Development Program and that of the Government of Ontario through the Ontario Media Development Corporation's Ontario Book Initiative. We further acknowledge the support of the Canada Council for the Arts and the Ontario Arts Council for our publishing program.

ANCIENT FOREST
FRIENDLY

Typeset in Garamond by M&S, Toronto
Printed and bound in Canada

McClelland & Stewart Ltd.
75 Sherbourne Street
Toronto, Ontario
M5A 2P9
www.mcclelland.com/NCL

1 2 3 4 5   14 13 12 11 10

DEEP HOLLOW CREEK

ONE

Her eyes, Stella thought, were the colour of Spanish mahogany, but they lacked the lustre of organic fibre. The soul had gone out of the wood, had dissipated. What was life, she asked herself, that the soul could escape so. She had come into the valley to find life for herself. It is not difficult, she thought, to recall all the fine things which have been written about life. She could summon to witness Taylor's rose, Browne's flame, and Harvey's microcosmic sun, the palpitating radiance of the life-streak seen with the naked eye in the egg of a barnyard fowl. With inevitable logic her mind pursued the theme from generation to decay, for about death, too, fine things had been written. But death – short as the circuit between cradle and grave – presumed life; and the flame, however thin, must be lit before it can be blown out by the thousand unsuspected gusts noted by the compilers and annotators, and amassers of vital statistics within the universal bills of mortality.

Rose stood at the door with a jug of hot water.

You get this every morning, she said. You use cold at night.

Stella took the jug and placed it in the grey-white basin. The room was completely square. Beside the iron bedstead Rose's husband had placed the trunk and the box of books Stella had brought with her to eke out the experience she hoped to have. At the end of the bed was a purple quilt come fresh from the hands of Eaton's or Simpsons packers. On a wooden table stood a coal-oil lamp. Stella pulled the trunk across the six-inch floor boards to make a seat at the window. The window was a narrow oblong pane set vertically in a hinged frame which hooked up to the low ceiling. The trunk dragged under it provided a seat from which she could smell the air sharp with sage – no more. She could see nothing. The house was set under the hill and between the window and the gravel bank there was a space only a few feet wide – a narrow track – wide enough to trap a cow or to let the house dog slink through to the brow of the hill.

From beyond the wooden door came the noise of the family at breakfast – the clink of the frying-pan, the scraping of benches, the ring of spoon or fork on plate, an occasional grunt or the quick querulous voice of a child and the sudden silence following a half-audible hist.

You can have yours, Rose had said to Stella, when they get out.

No doubt Stella's being there, despite the tenacity with which Sam, the husband, had fought for the privilege, had complicated the ordinary domestic routine. Sam had been quite frank. The privilege was a matter of board. Arriving at the station to fetch Stella the day before, he had made his announcement with toneless finality:

When Mockett said to me you haven't got the room you got six children, I said it's my turn and I'm not going to be fooled any longer. You had the last and you had the one before that and the girl that married old Buzzard's foreman. I've had none since Mr. Jones. It's my turn to have her – and here I am to get you. The kids are sleeping up and Mrs. Sam Flower, he mentioned the name defiantly, has got the room all fixed. I brought her down for the ride. Don't believe what he tells you. He's one of hers at the stopping house and she makes a fool of him and Bill and the whole lot of them. Come with me.

Are you the brother the school secretary wrote about, Stella asked, looking at the grey curls which reached tendrils from under the inner edge of the brim of his small black felt hat.

His thin features tightened.

If he wrote against me that's me – if he said that you could stay at the stopping house that's Bill and her and him too and the others.

It was Rose's eyes that Stella had first noticed. Between the shocks of stiff brown hair, which branched from under the circle of an orange tam-o'-shanter, lay the eyes. Only the tam-o'-shanter glowed in the sunlight, with mock vitality. Rose was standing at the edge of the dusty road waiting to be picked up. She wore a blue cotton dress, brown cotton stockings, and a pair of flat-heeled rubber-soled shoes.

It's her, Sam said, as she climbed into the back seat of the car, pulling by the hand a child in a white organdy dress. The child's face was hidden by its roughly cut hair. Its feet, cased in black patent leather slippers, shuffled on the step.

Stella had looked about as the car crossed the bridge, which was balanced like a plank across the river. The hill rose on the other side – brown banks, dust-greyed sagebrush, and yellowed grass on the sheering, off-rolling hills.

This here, said Sam, was the old stage road. Freight went up and down here, hauled by horses. Then they brought camels, they did.

He glared defiance.

Shod 'em, he went on. The beasts should of done in the dry heat. They should of done, but they didn't. Couldn't stand the stones and lonesomeness.

Mrs. Sam said nothing.

We ran the first cars here, he said. We ran them – me and my brother-in-law, him as was husband to my sister before she left him and began to live with him who lives now with Bill and her at the stopping house.

They were fine cars too, he said, but that's not the point now. It's trucks. I just get my truck and he writes to the government and takes the contract for hauling mail and other things away for themselves. Now they live fine at the House.

High up the road wound. Below on the left the river flowed between reddish banks – flat to the eye's sheer vertical. To the right stretched sand and sagebrush and gilded lifeless grass. Around the corner, over the bank – this way and that – balls of withered Russian thistle crept in the warm breeze like giant spiders.

Tumble-weed – snorted Sam Flower, as he flattened out a ball with his wheel. Made by the Almighty with the prime and only purpose of scaring a finicky mare.

The rest had been silence. Up hill – the road crumbling away at the shoulder – they climbed, close into the bank, with a sudden jerk of the wheel as the red hood of a truck rounded the corner wheels close to the inner bank. All else tended to the river-like artery which twisted below as the land sloped off – fell off roughly – tumbled stones down. All things converged to it. Only the car climbed tenaciously up the slope, challenging God's providence and the laws of gravitation.

Breakfast was obviously over. The door slammed, feet rounded the corner of the house. There was a tap on the door.

You can have yours now, Rose said. I didn't get it, not knowing what you'd want.

Stella scanned the domestic debris – greasy plates streaked with egg, bits of scorched fried potato.

Toast, she said. All I ever have is toast.

Rose cut slices off the loaf. Stella could see only the browned crust. When she ate she knew that something had gone wrong with the working of the yeast. The bread had soured in the bottle. The bread was cold and grey and sour. Only the surface had been charred a little on the flat rack over the flame.

Every morning as Stella washed she heard the scraping in the kitchen. Every morning she ate her toast while Rose stood behind her at the stove fingering the handle of the granite coffee pot. Every morning when she had finished her breakfast Rose swept up the crumbs and threw them to the chickens and cut more bread to pack in pails for the lunches. Every day at noon the children unpacked their pails in the space behind the partition in the schoolhouse. They accepted the bread as they accepted what Stella taught them, without comment.

The bread, Stella thought, was Rose's peculiar emblem – the emblem of a failure which Rose's sister-in-law Mamie Flower let no one forget.

———

Can the validity of this emblem – or of any other emblem – she wondered, be assessed. I see the hand, the compass, the dragon when the book falls open. The hand reaches over the ledge spilling one knows not what of essence or substance into the narrow cleft. Through Sassetta's eyes or Edmund Spenser's I see in the shadow of Limbo the red cross – and they see it because the light glances off and reflects from the fire which warms their shoulders as they work. I have always taken the compass as a thing to be held. Yet the hand falters measuring the fleeting body of flame.

Any day looking from Sam's house on the hill, Stella could see the angled roof of the stopping house diagonally to the right against the downfalling drop of the land which she thought seemed to contract and fall into the narrow valley from the flat outreaching land above. Only with difficulty, she thought, can I raise my eyes. They focus inevitably on the stopping house – the inn at which, after the fashion of the country, one may stop for the payment of a fee – one may stop, she thought, if one is merely a traveller or a salesman with his commodity and not, in the nature of the now and here, more than a momentary commodity himself.

Over at the stopping house Rose's sister-in-law would shake a knowing head. Arranging and rearranging the folds of black crepe to show a slim city-bred ankle, Mamie Flower measured Rose's failure by her own success.

Mamie tells her story, Stella thought, with the abandoned fluency of the lady of quality in Smollett's – or was it in Defoe's tale.

––––

6

Sam married one of the local girls, Mamie would say. A peculiar lot they were – she and those before her. Poor Rose, she would say, she knowing no more than to let Sam have her. And that's how she came here and that's how she's lived. Sam was a fine boy. Old Pa Flower intended him for me, he being the oldest. When he wrote mother, he said, send the girlie for a visit. All the way from Hull it was. Old Ma Flower had gone to school with my mother long ago and after Pa Flower had made his way here with Ma Flower he brought her back to Hull for a visit, collecting tracts, picking up this and that to offset the way Pa made his money with the bar and the credit and the men herded along the river panning out gold and thinking of the New Jerusalem. I was brought up with chapel folk, too, but I plagued my mother till she let me learn to dance, and it was my dancing and my littleness, not five feet – patting her blonde curled hair, tightening a pearl bob in her ear – it was my dancing and littleness that made Bill gape.

He was the youngest, she said, of Adam Flower's three boys. He wasn't intended in the invitation. But I knew he would mould more easily than Sam. Sam had his cars and had had his girls before – and the threat of Rose's father, though I didn't know then. It's to be Bill, I decided, and we can take his share of Pa's money and go back to London and in London the money and Bill's six feet of handsome muscle will go a long way. Sam, she said, was smaller and thin. I'll brush Bill and comb him and take him out of his dungarees and put him in good blue Yorkshire woven serge, Sunday and weekday the like.

That was when Sam was running the taxis for the men. There was money everywhere – creeks vomiting money, men throwing it in heaps on the counter, too lazy to count it. Bill's sister had just been married here to the bank clerk from the Rock. Pa had sent hands out on horses all over the country asking people to come. Minnie's husband, Bernard, had given up banking and had started his own business with the cars – he and Sam. Mockett was Pa's clerk – worth anything to him in the store, weighing out the tea, sending for supplies, adding up the bills. Mockett never liked Bernard but he did like Minnie. I'll stand behind her, he said, when that porcupine sheds his quills; and he did and he had his neck broken for the doing. But that's another story. Dick Mockett was my own sister-in-law's so-called husband for a while and now she's gone to eat her bread in bitterness and Dick's still here weighing out tea, cooking when I can't get a girl from the reserve, milking the cow, and Sam's sold out to us and he has the prick of his Rose always in his thumb.

I was only the daughter of Ma Flower's friend then – asked here because Ma Flower's conscience was heavy under the thought of what whisky money might do to her boys. When Pa wrote, she wrote too. Send Mamie, she wrote, so that Sam can marry a God-fearing chapel girl, daughter to a friend of my blessed youth. Send a light into Egypt – to this heathen continent – to light the delusion of my first born.

My mother was a little uneasy. I wasn't the straight burning flame that Ma Flower wanted. There was my dancing to account for. My sister, Hannah, would have been a better choice but she was already married to a man of some means. Despite her chapel ways Hannah had married a man with a big house and a grand piano. I played the piano too and danced, and my mother thought that the money she had spent on me would bring better returns in a foreign market. So little Mamie was sent across the Atlantic – across a whole vacant continent to marry a man on the outer rim. As I said, I didn't intend to stay in this deep hollow valley after I married – but I didn't have my whole way then.

I married Bill and Pa didn't make the same fuss as he had for Minnie or as he would have for Sam. I was married, a stranger in a strange country, and I've been here ever since – not like the rest.

Just after I married Bill, Sam came creeping home with Rosie. Bernard had gone and there was nothing but debt on the cars. Pa Flower took it well enough. Take your share, he said to Sam, the middle half of the whole long stretch. Your brother Reg has taken his share by the river. Take your stretch and build your house and raise your get. But Ma thought of how the Lord's hand was heavy because of the whisky money.

Things everywhere were beginning to crack. The men weren't buying as they did. We couldn't go to England just then, Pa Flower said. He'd only Bill now to depend on. Pa gave Bill money though and we went to the coast for our honeymoon.

I used to dance for Bill in the evenings and he would lie on the bed staring as if he somehow had got a thing too precious to touch. Mamie's so little, he used to say. Mamie's so little – why she's the littlest woman in the whole goddam country. Sam's Rosie was big-boned and dull. Sam took her off quietly in one of the cars he'd salvaged so that the baby could be born out of Ma's sight. The doctor told Sam then that she was twisted inside as she was flat and square-boned out. Take my advice, he said, and let it be the last. But there were five more and each time Sam took her out.

Apart from that, she said to Stella, she's not been off the place except when he took her this time to pick you up. Why, only Sam knows. He said to Bill, She's not been off the place for some time. Since it's my turn certain I'll take her to see her sister.

———

Always the story came. The variations were only those inspired by the moment. The story was part of the fabric of their lives.

Rosie, Mamie Flower would say compassionately, is not really quite right here – her little hand with its pink nails resting near the tight curled fringe from under which her eyes moved greenly, restlessly.

Poor girl, she would say. I'd do anything to make life easier for her but she won't have anything to do with me. Somehow you'd think I'd hurt her. Her children, now, come here often. They find it pleasant here. Gladys doesn't like being at home; there's nothing pretty there.

She would gaze at the white woodwork in the private parlour, the gleaming nickel on the Franklin heater, the chintz and lace on the windows, the orange and green fantasy on the polished linoleum floor.

My men change for dinner, she would say, white shirts all of them – even Mockett, out of his apron into his white shirt. Even a girl like Gladys can see the difference. I told Sam to get her things at the Rock. I taught her how to file her nails and I trimmed her hair for her. Rose doesn't like it. She sent her back with a lace blouse I gave her. But it's all here, she said to Stella, raising her hand, keeping it raised to tighten the bob on her ear. Like little shells, she said. Bill says they're like little shells. Bill says he has the littlest woman and the biggest place on the whole creek.

Everyone comes here, she would say, rocking a little in her chair. What Sam wanted to do digging himself up into the hill I don't know. There was to be another house later, he said; but there wasn't and there won't be. Every cent he gets he spends on cows and horses – every cent.

No one goes to see Rose, she would say. No one.

―――

Round the valley the hills crowded. Rà'tltem the Shuswaps had
called their village there; they were the people of the deep
hollow. In the jack-pine the dusky grouse, the ruffed grouse, the
sharp-tailed grouse hid away from the hunters in the autumn.
On the branches, in the pools of light on the bleached and terra
cotta hillside, the red-eyed, speckle-coated fool-hens sat unconcerned, waiting for their necks to be wrung without the trouble
of a shot. Crossing the rock pile, with a rattle of quilts, the
porcupine stripped bark from the trees. Antoine Billy's boy saw
a cougar in a canyon. Sometimes a moose crossed the creek
with a great breaking and cracking of twigs – a face solemn and
bearded as a patriarch thrust through the brittle branches. Out
from the edge of the hill the land rolled in ridges dotted and
streaked with the white rimmed alkali lakes. Out on the range
hills the cattle moved   Bill's with Sam's, Sam's with Reg's.
Only the brand made the distinction when, in the fall, the
brothers joined forces from necessity to round them up, herding
them here into the corral, cutting them out there, driving them
off to their separate feed lots.

In the valley all things moved to a point. The road ran
into the creek both ways to the stopping house – though, if
one stood on the hill where the water broke in the spring,
one could see the road winding like a thread the whole
length of the valley. No one stood on the hill. In the valley
one spoke of the road running up or down, into or out of
the centre. The private parlour, and the public parlour where
the Indians stood shuffling their feet waiting patiently for
Mockett to take off his apron, to come from his cow, to fold
up his copy of the *Manchester Guardian* and to unlock the
store, weighing out tea, weighing out flour, pouring out
coal-oil, sorting out mail – here was the centre. Here people

came from choice or necessity. Here came the proud and the meek. Here came everyone except Rose.

I would starve on this hill, Rose said one day to Stella, rather than go there. Thank God Sam built up here – up under the hill. If you go up to the top, she said, you can look down away from it – down to the river, across to the great folds and twists on the other side.

What did she tell you? she asked, her glance thrusting for a moment down to the house in the valley, cutting through the logs, searching out Mamie. What did she say down there?

The quilt, she went on sullenly, I sent for to Eaton's. There's something soft about purple-coloured quilts. She won't stay with you, Bill said to Sam about you. Even your kids like it best down here. Did she show you something when Sam took you down? she asked. Did she show you the room Mr. Thompson had? I said to Sam the table would make a good big desk. I told him you can't hope to do it. I pay the most taxes, he said, I have the most kids.

Mockett writes to the government, she said. He says we have ten kids – three from the river, two of hers, and five of ours ready. If it wasn't for our five there wouldn't be a school and her boys could do like the rest. So the government says it's a school and Mockett has himself made secretary and we have to send our five. If I don't board the teacher, Sam says, I'll take my five out and see what happens to the school. Then Mr. Duke, the inspector, comes down from the Rock and says, Sam it's no use, if you don't send your five the law will exact it of you. There's fines and there's punishments and penalties for such. Mockett's a good fellow, he says. He's got brains. He knows what's best. That's the only time Duke came here. Every year he comes. Every year he eats and plays down there. Only once he came to tell Sam that the law could make him pay the most taxes because he had the most kids. I wouldn't go near the place, she said, not even if I starved. You can't keep the kids away. It's natural they want to go.

She emptied the pan of dishwater into the flume. Chickens came round the corner of the house, pecked and jostled, balanced on the edge of the trough, dipped for this, fluttered in and scratched automatically on the greasy boards. The water gurgled away over the little dip, leaving a trail of slime behind it.

I've got some nice things too, she said. But I'm not putting them for everyone to see. I've got some boudoir shoes, she said, and I'm not beholding to Sam for them either. My aunt gave me the money for my birthday a long time ago. I had it put by for a long time. Then I saw them in the catalogue. They're purple, she said, like the quilt and they got feathers on the front like a curl of ostrich plumes.

She wiped her hands on the sides of her cotton dress as she went towards a box high up on the shelf in the corner – behind the box of shoeing nails, the pile of horseshoes tied together with a piece of rope, the box of buckles, the box of rivets.

The only trouble, she said, the only thing – when they did send them they had to go and send a pair that didn't fit, and somehow I just never got time to send them back.

Rose's eyes were dull cork. Even her branching hair resisted the morning light.

No animating fire within, no reflection of the sun outside, Stella thought, yet somewhere there is life – somewhere there must be fire burning inward, letting the ash drop on the source of fire itself. But still, she thought, what is this fire. And again – by what refraction can one know flame . . .

I like to go places too, Rose said. Six times Sam took me out – six times from here to the hospital. Reg's wife had hers by the river without anyone – Reg saying nothing, going in the snow to get old Susannah from the reserve, passing right by her own sister's door, mine, going round the hill to avoid the stopping house, Rose said – jerking her head towards the valley – then arriving back too late. Six times Sam took me out to have his kids respectable in a hospital bed. Up to the Rock she goes – her glance turned to the house in the valley – the littlest woman in the whole country, to the stampede dance, to sit in the shop to have her hair frizzed, playing the piano and dancing and coming back in a fainting condition, all wore out so that Mockett has to carry her up to bed, sitting in bed all winter in her lace negligee with Bill in a clean shirt holding her hand. So little and so weak, he told Sam, just like a doll propped up on her pillows – Mockett emptying her slop pail, the honour of emptying it all his own.

I never asked Sam to take me anywhere, she said, except once. They'd all been. Every one of them had been to Green Lake. It's up on the hill about eighteen miles from here. In the spring they go to picnics there. I asked Sam, she said, to take me there too. I asked him, she said, and he did. But then, she said – looking at Stella steadily – but then he had to go and take me when the leaves was off the trees.

TWO

Some things were to happen before Stella left Sam's house and the view of the bleak folds of brown earth across the river.

Don't ever drink the river water, Rose said. Everyone who drinks it comes back here to die.

The river, Stella learned, was a sly subtle serpent, the flick of gold under its smooth belly. Those who stroked the belly, who let the hand slip and wander under the smooth folds, were bitten for their pain. When the river failed, the miners came to the creeks. They built a town of shacks down in the bottom, where the people of the deep creek lived. They came and they stayed for a while and the country beat them. They put their hands on the gold and the gold burned like the taste of whisky. They put their hands on the women and the earth folded about their feet and the curves of the land took them on so that they never came back.

Up behind the flats, Rose said, there's a lake. Nicholas Farish told me. He's not to be believed – talking and laughing, laughing and talking. He comes to help Sam with the hay. You'll see him, she said, about. He knows the Indians. He traded his way into the country, coming with a car over the Burnt Ground Hill, making a deal for a team and a wagon as soon as he came. He knows horses almost better than Sam. He has an eye for ring-bone and side-bone and spavin, Sam says. He puts his hand on a horse and he knows. He knows too much for one who wasn't born here, she said. She down there at the House doesn't like him and no wonder. I don't mind him myself. He means no harm. He knows there are other roads but one. He told me, she said, sitting at this very table, his black hat laying on his knee and his great bat-winged chaps shining with conchas – he told me what he'd seen. He was out looking for a white stallion. They'd all seen it but no man had branded it. He got off to have a sleep and when he got off he left the bay he rode standing on the lines. When he woke up, the horse had moved off and going to look for him he came plumb on it – a great black lake. You couldn't see the lake, he said, only the edge falling off. And when he went to look he lay flat, for the edge went down and down to the black water. There was ledges and on the ledges there was bushes and flying over the water down in the cleft was birds and the land about him was dry and hard and there was nothing coming into the lake and nothing going out. He said for a minute he thought his horse had got in. But it was the wise old bay his wife rides. And then he saw the ears moving along behind a ridge on the other side. He says he never could find that lake again. But the Indians know it, he says, and talk about it in their own houses. They have a god, he says – one called Coyote. But I can't, he said, say more, Mrs. Flower. They trust me and they tell me but there's reasons why a man can't say more. Then he puts on his hat and fools with the kid and off he goes. He's the only person who calls me that, she said, Mrs. Flower's mine by right. Sam's the oldest. But it's Mrs. Sam or Rose and the name goes slipping where it's not due. Nicholas Farish can see when a person's stealing what's not hers.

Sometimes Nicholas Farish brought whispers of strange things. Sometimes a child on the hill spied someone coming or going.

– They're expecting some mail down to the river. They're driving old Aggie up in the cart.

– There's a new car. It's perhaps the post inspector.

Let Mockett add them up straight, said Sam to Stella, while she keeps him talking in the parlour.

The most fruitful source of news, however, was the telephone.

You can listen there to a whole country you can't see – Gladys, Sam's girl, said.

Mrs. Sparrow's kid up to Napoleon Creek is sick, Stella heard them say. She's calling the doctor. I can't come till tomorrow, he says, or the next day. I've three babies coming. You can't hurry them, Mrs. Sparrow. Nature is nature. Keep her in bed, he says, and give her a teaspoon of oil. Open the bowels, he says, and mind, Mrs. Sparrow, no hot-cakes, no ripe tomatoes. A thin diet, Mrs. Sparrow.

He don't come easy, not Old Grafter, said Sam, turning from the instrument.

One night Sam had a story to tell at supper. The youngsters reached for the yellow, sweating butter, dipped forks into the bowl of potatoes, passed plates for a moist pink slab of pickled meat.

Williams up at the Three Forks had been done in. Sam had heard it on the phone when he came in from feeding the horses. He had been following Williams's affairs for some days. Steers weren't selling well. Three and a half cents on the hoof for prime winter-grained three year olds. A man might as well hold for a year if he could. Four year olds brought a little less but there was no expense if a man could put up enough hay on his own place. Sam's old bread-loaf stack from last year hadn't been touched yet. Williams had to sell though. The Three Forks was a tough spot. You couldn't coax the water from the river. The hay ripened only once. The one crop depended on the spring rains. The range land was poor and the hoppers got more than the steers. Williams had to sell. His boy had been hurt in an accident. He'd been sent out. Then they sent him back. They had done all they could and they couldn't do more. He had come back the day before Williams had left with the drive – brought up on the train, then freighted in. The train they all agreed was a milk train right enough though only Sam had ever travelled it.

You'll see when you go on it. You'll see what I saved you, Sam said to Stella, when I fetched you up from below.

Williams had made his deal with the buyer. At least the buyer had said to bring the steers over. It wasn't business to buy on the place. Steers could only be judged after the drive.

If you've fed them good, he had said, and bring them easy, you'll stand a chance with the others.

Sam had heard him on the phone. He had heard the Three Forks ring and he had listened and he had heard Williams say – If I bring them and you don't take them I'm through. Men should be careful on the phone, Sam said. Men shouldn't trumpet their secret thoughts to the whole country. The only thing a phone's good for is to listen. That's why I pay the price, he said. You can listen all evening if you have a mind. But for business a man has to be close and secret.

I ride out, said Sam to Stella, they'd drive their beef in

first. They'd underbid you on the half cent. They'd cut logs down in your way. They'd turn the river up-hill.

He glared down through the darkness into the valley.

It was bad luck – he said, falling from anger to contemplation – it was bad luck that the river hadn't been turned up-hill for Williams.

From Williams's ranch to the yards was a long drive. He had no boys to help so he had to use hired hands to bring the beasts out. Hired hands and steers don't team well. The hands ride them too hard. Steers are easily fretted. They know those they can trust and they don't trust casual hands. There would be nowhere where Williams could water them. The country would be dry like a bleached bone. A little rain would have helped. But then again it wouldn't. Nature had no common sense. When it rained it rained until the road was a bog hole of gumbo. It would take Williams four days to bring the steers in. Each night riding herd on them he must have watched the flesh dropping away. The steers from that range have no bottom. They can't hold their weight. There would be no place he could stop to water them before he got to the yards – to fill their bellies with water so that they could tip the scales a little higher after they had been left overnight to shrink.

It wouldn't have made any difference though. Williams didn't have a chance to get them on the scales. There was plenty of cattle there. The buyer could pick and choose.

They're skeletons, he said. I'm not buying bone.

You'll take them, Williams said, and pay me the current rate. I'm not hiring men and driving beasts here for you to make a fool of me. I'm not a mink-rancher, he said, I raise ordinary marketable beasts for ordinary men. These are marketable beasts. You needn't think you can phone me to bring them out and then laugh in my face.

Sell them to the bone dealer, said the buyer. I told you you could take your chance with the others.

I heard Jo Creech telling his brother, Sam said, that Williams didn't stop. He walked right across the road into the hotel room he'd spoken for for the night and he pulled out the old Colt he used for sniping coyotes and that was the end of him. Now at the yards they don't know what to do with his cattle. They phoned Mrs. Williams to come. I can't, she said, I can't leave the boy. Send someone in so that I can come out. And now they've got the cattle and they've got Williams's body and his horse. When a man goes away quiet and takes his losses nobody cares. A man's got no right to make a public nuisance of himself, said Sam.

A dead body's an awful thing in this country now, said George, Sam's boy. Summer the ground's baked hard as nails. Winters she's froze. When old McIntosh died they had to put him in a tree out of the coyotes' way until the ground thawed in the spring. Heat and cold between them gets the best of things.

THREE

Before school opened Stella had gone with Sam on an official visit to Mockett. At the same time Sam had taken her to pay her respects to the lady at the House. He seemed to have timed this meeting with all the precision one would use in sighting a gun on a sitting grouse. Or perhaps he had studied Mrs. Bill Flower's habits and knew them as well as he knew those of any horse in his own stable. He knocked on the door of the public parlour, opened it according to custom, and went in. Mamie Flower was standing by the door of the inner parlour wrapped in a mauve padded dressing gown, her hair in pin-curls. She raised her hand to her head as she turned to escape. Sam closed the door behind them. She stood poised on the door-sill – stood tightening the pearl ring in her ear. Then she came forward.

I asked you to bring her to tea at four, she said. You are a little early.

I milk the cows at four, Sam said, always at four. Today I milk them at four as I did yesterday and will do tomorrow. There's other business besides school business. Now is as good a time as four is for you to meet her.

They sat down in silence for a few minutes.

We always have tea at four, Mamie said. We have our dinner late so that the men have time to change. Mr. Thompson liked having tea at four. He said it was a luxury he never thought he would enjoy on a cattle ranch. He was a very sociable man. In the evening he joined us around the piano. He enjoyed life here with us. He liked it best in the House talking to me or playing cribbage with Dick Mockett but he was always equal to a hunting trip with Bill and the boys.

Sam shuffled one foot back and forth on the floor and looked into the lace which covered the window. Stella could just see the shadow of someone moving across to the barn.

I am sure Rose is making you comfortable, Mamie said to Stella. But since Sam is so busy perhaps you would like to go up the hill with our boys on Sunday.

We've got plans of going up the hill ourselves on Sunday, said Sam, and it's about time we pushed off now. We have to drop in at the store to see Mockett before we go.

The school is Dick Mockett's school really, said Mamie Flower, turning from Sam. In the bad days when we lived on the Porcupine, when the boys were just babies and I saw no one but Indian women, Dick Mockett would ride up when he'd made up the accounts for Pa Flower.

He used to keep the stones wore off flat like the rocks in the creek bottom, didn't he, Sam said. Didn't want you to feel lonely so far from home when Bill was away, did he.

Her hand straightened a fold of her dressing gown.

Dick Mockett was always kind, she said. He comes from Lancashire so we really weren't from the same country but there are things that we both understand.

She addressed herself to Stella.

At any rate, don't worry, he used to say. Your boys won't grow up ignorant. We'll see to that. When they're ready for school we'll have a school. And he wrote to Victoria and he found things out and we used to sit planning it.

Stella tried to see it – the Porcupine and Mamie with two small children, one a baby perhaps in her arms. She could see nothing but the enamelled nails straightening the folds of mauve cloth.

Dick Mockett was always kind, Mamie said, and he's been particular too, he has. The government will pay so much, he said, and the rest we can raise by local taxes. Nothing but a B.A. would satisfy Dick. He's built a good library in the school – not that our boys need it since we have books here. We have a whole wall of books in the other room.

Sam got up.

Remember, Mockett is the one who knows about the school, Mamie said, knows everything to the very last detail.

It was not until the minister came that Stella saw Mamie Flower again. When Mr. Ellicot came from the Rock Mrs. Bill Flower entertained. Everyone came – at least all who could be reasonably expected to come. The Farishes came from the Porcupine, the homestead which Bill had staked out while he waited for old Pa Flower to die. He and Mamie had lived at the House with its bar and its store and its barn for a little while after they had come from their coast honeymoon. But Pa Flower had insulted Mamie.

The story of the insult could be had for the listening.

The morning after they got back from their honeymoon Mamie had risen early despite the fatigue of her journey in. She had risen to get breakfast as Pa Flower had suggested it was the business of his boy's wife to do. She had gone to the garden at the side of the house and had picked flowers and put them in a bowl on the table. She had rummaged in Ma's drawers until she found a cloth to cover the oil-cloth on the table. She had picked out the thinnest cups she could find.

In the kitchen the girl who did for Ma was making hot-cakes and frying steak. Mamie shivered as she had shivered when she first came. But she knew how to let well enough alone. She felt a little queasy but she mastered her nausea and rang the bell for the men.

Pa didn't notice a thing when he came in. He sat where he always sat and the girl brought his plate of hot-cakes and steak. Mamie poured the coffee. Ma was ailing then and hadn't come down yet. She was feeling the weight of the whisky money and the worry of its flowing a little less freely too. Pa Flower said nothing. Bill ate in silence as he always did. Then it happened. Down on the edge of his cup Pa brought his spoon with a noisy clatter. Mamie looked up. Pa sat there pounding and glaring. Mamie looked at Bill, who just kept on eating, folding his cakes over, cutting through so butter ran out of the gash. Pa pounded again.

It's his coffee, said Bill. He wants his coffee filled.

Mamie stared at Pa. Then she left the table and from that day on the girl that did for Ma got the whole of Pa's breakfast.

Later on Bill tried to make Pa see that Mamie wasn't like the other girls. She wasn't hard and callous like Sam's Rose for instance. She had set her mind on having her baby in England and, sitting in bed with the tears making her eyes soft and appealing, she had told Bill how she'd dreamed that she would die if she stayed in the valley and had said how when the baby was born she would dance for him again. She felt oppressed in the House, she said, because of the way Pa had acted.

Pa was amazed, Bill said, when he spoke to him.

Whenever, he said, did a man ask for coffee in any other way.

He was sorry that Ma had written to her old school friend.

No woman's got a right to have feelings, he said. There is a word every woman should write in her prayer book on the very front page and that word is endurance. It's a suffering world, he said, for everyone, and a woman must take her share.

Now Rose – he said. But Bill cut him short.

If you breathe my wife's pure name with hers, Bill said, I'll stake out my own place up the creek and you can get Sam to work like a slave for you.

Pa didn't say anything. Then Bill went up the creek and staked out his own place and had logs cut and started building a house. And Mamie said just how she wanted an arch here and window there.

It's terribly hard to build an arch, Bill said.

I've set my mind on it, she said. It will be smart and neat, not like this old barn of a house.

She didn't think then how lonely she would be and how little an arch would mean with only the Indians to gawk at it.

Pa didn't take Bill seriously for a while. But Bill kept on building. Out of some money he'd saved he got the doors and the window-frames and Mockett helped him in ways Pa didn't know. When Pa realized that Bill was in earnest he gave in.

Money's getting scarcer and scarcer, he said, but since you know what you want I'm not going to stand in your way. I left my father's shop in Lancashire and you can leave me here if you've the mind to do so. I've got no more land to give you yet but I'll get Mockett to make a draft on the bank at the Rock.

When Mamie heard about the draft she told Bill that there wasn't much time to lose.

Get Mockett to book a passage, she said. There's a new thing called twilight-sleep and I've set my mind on it.

So they went. But Bill didn't feel right the whole time they were away. There wasn't a steer anywhere not even among Madame Tussaud's wax-works. He was disappointed in the lions and scoffed at the way the soldiers rode.

The thing no one can tell me, he said, is that an Englishman knows how to ride a horse. It's the very last thing he knows how to do.

Mamie had thought she would keep Bill in England. But after a while she wasn't so sure. She felt herself a little lost in London. She had no importance at all. And when she met some of the girls she had known and saw the way they lived she was a little frightened. Pa's draft was melting away.

It was shocking, Sam said, what the baby had cost. Bill could have set himself up with a fine herd of cattle for less.

When Mamie spoke of their coming back, she said I chose to come and I chose to stay. That was all.

When they came back Bill took her up through the valley to the Porcupine, which Mockett had prepared, only stopping long enough at Pa's house to show the baby in its long lace dress – the baby unwrapped from the white rabbit blanket Mockett had sent it when it was born.

Now the Farishes lived at the Porcupine which had stood vacant for a long time after Pa Flower had died leaving no will so that Bill had had to buy off Sam and Reg.

How dimly the light filters through the broken fragments gathered carelessly, pieced together when the sharp edges set in motion the curious workings of the fancy, Stella thought. A few pieces gathered the night Mr. Ellicot had come, Mamie's endless commentary, Myrtle Farish's opaque candour.

No through-light scarves here, she thought. Their bodies wrap them like horse blankets. And why, she asked, must Swift conspire with Donne to mock my pen as it writes. Shall I set sail in a boat of yahoo skins or sit weaving a bracelet of bright hair.

Myrtle Farish, Nicholas's wife, had been a school teacher. Mamie always spoke of her as that poor little thing. Anyone who was married to Nicholas Farish deserved sympathy.

The hours the poor little thing must spend by herself, Mamie said, while that man rides about the country making friends of the Indians. It's not as if there weren't people here, she said.

Myrtle painted and sang and danced and would have played the piano too if there had been a piano to play. She seemed quite happy with Nicholas Farish. They had no children but shared their lot with a buff-coloured Chesapeake bitch named Flossie. Flossie never left the Porcupine. She guarded the saddles hanging in the barn, chased away rats, and, Sam said, looked with suspicion at all who passed up and down the road.

Bill Flower, Mamie reported, riding home late one night down the road, had heard gramophone music and through the windows of the Porcupine had seen Nicholas and Myrtle dancing just as if they had been on the floor of the stampede dance-hall up at the Rock. He felt that there was something unnatural about it. Mamie's dancing was in a class by itself. When she danced he just sat and looked.

They all danced together of course on church night after Mr. Ellicot had said the prayers and preached his sermon in the music room which opened out of the private parlour. Even Dick Mockett danced, leading off Mamie in a measured revolving circle after she and Bill had danced the hesitation waltz to the tune of the Merry Widow. Mamie had taught Gladys to dance and George too. Sam's children came to the service though Sam came seldom and Rose not at all. George danced with every muscle taut, his arms and legs moving like pistons. He had, Mamie said, no sense of rhythm.

Between Mamie and Mr. Ellicot there was a strong bond of union. And to the pair Mockett was linked by a tenuous strand. They were all of them exiles.

I was brought up with chapel people, Mamie said, but for the time being I am a good Anglican for Mr. Ellicot's sake. After all the Anglican church is the national church. We are all Anglicans by birth.

In the afternoon Mr. Ellicot arrived. In the evening he changed from the tweed suit in which he had driven down into his official black. After he had shaken hands with the guests as they arrived he buttoned on his cassock and spoke to them in the music room.

I come, said Mr. Ellicot, to bring the word of God to whoever will listen. Let us not be too serious about it. We will pray and I will speak to you for a little while and we will enjoy Mrs. Flower's famous hospitality. There is good will and friendship in a gathering of this kind which makes us one communion for the time being.

Sam, who had come to bring Stella and to return her to the house on the hill, shuffled his feet and looked from under lowered lids towards Mamie who was seated at the piano ready to strike out the notes of the first hymn.

I think, whispered Myrtle Farish, who had been seated next to Stella, that of all the local group I am the only baptized Anglican here.

Up on the hill, Stella thought, Rose is sitting by herself. Only the smallest of her six children is with her. No one had asked her to come to church, to be sure.

You can wash and dress if you like, she had said at supper. Their church is only an excuse for parties and dancing. If God takes notice of anybody as little as her all this washing and white shirts and dancing will only bring harm where there's enough already. Mockett is at the bottom of it all.

Mr. Ellicot prayed. Everyone, Stella noticed, posed in uncomfortable posture. Mamie, spared, bowed over the keys. To sit stolidly in the chair no doubt was to enter too little into the spirit of good will and fellowship. It was to condemn the ritual by which man lives and moves. Sam sat. The rest twisted uncomfortably in the unaccustomed pose. Only Myrtle Farish looked comfortable.

I could play the hymns, she whispered, but I wasn't asked.

Mamie struck a chord. Mockett had passed out hymn books. Mamie's voice rang shrill over the rattle of the piano keys –

> We plough the fields and scatter
>> The good seed on the land;
> But it is fed and watered
>> By God's almighty hand.

> He sends the frost in winter . . .

Mockett was seized with a fit of coughing. He buried his head against the chair-back in front of him. Nicholas Farish edged close to Myrtle and muttered something about Mrs. Hawkins.

———

Frost was already in the air. Stella had watched it turn the leaves of the cottonwood trees in the creek bottom into flat yellow discs. By day the sun shone warm and the butter sweated on the table and the cream soured in the flat pans on the pantry shelf. The water was running low in the creek.

From spring until summer, from summer until spring they had said it was always a question of water. Sam hauled his house water with a team from a spring on the hill. He used water from the creek to irrigate his hay. Bill had first rights on the creek water, then Sam, then Mrs. Hawkins, who had come in from Arizona with an aged husband, a young partner, and a herd of long-horned cattle. She had bought the old Buzzard ranch and with the ranch went the third water rights. Nicholas Farish had no rights at all. He rented the Porcupine from Bill for his army pension of ten dollars a month. One week out of every four or five when the mail came in Mockett would hand out the long envelope and Farish would open it and sign the slip and pass it across the counter to Mockett. For the rest they lived as they could and in spring living had resolved itself into an endless battle with Mrs. Hawkins.

Nicholas with Myrtle's help had planted a large garden. Further up the creek as the altitude increased nothing grew. The Porcupine stood just within the circle of God's pasture. Williams had lived in the desert, in the Egypt of locusts and drought.

Farish had planted his garden in the spring. Every night he went down with a spade and turned streams of water from the creek into the tunnels which ran between the rows of potatoes, cabbage, and corn. Above him on the creek the beavers worked. He would ride with an axe to the beaver dam and cut it away and the beavers would come out of their hiding and build again, cutting and hauling and plastering the logs together.

I wish my mother had dreamed about beavers, he said, then the beaver would be my manitou. It would have saved me a great deal of trouble. I wonder who fought the beavers before we came. Bill must have come himself or sent one of the boys.

One day Mrs. Hawkins rode past on her low-slung grey mare. She had ridden up the creek to look for a cow which had strayed from the yard at the Buzzard. It was a hot spring day and in the morning Farish had not gone down with his shovel to turn the water out of the shallow ditches. Myrtle and Flossie were together in the garden when Mrs. Hawkins rode past.

You've a prosperous-looking patch there, Mrs. Hawkins said, climbing off her mare and resting her elbows and chin on the rail fence. Where did Farish learn to grow spuds without water? They need a little hilling though. I think I'll send my pardner up to have a look at the way you do it.

Back she climbed and rode off. Half an hour later she came down with the cow. In the afternoon when Myrtle was sitting on the hill with Flossie, sitting in a patch of sunlight looking up at the blue above the rising ridges, letting her glance slide down from ledge to ledge into the bottom of the valley, she saw Mrs. Hawkins ride back up the turn of the road. At the boundary fence of the Buzzard Mrs. Hawkins stopped and tied her mare to a post. As she disappeared into the underbrush Myrtle saw the sunlight glancing off something she carried over her shoulder.

She's going into the bottom with a spade, Myrtle said to Flossie.

The next day when Farish went down to the garden the water had been turned back into the creek. At the end of the first row of potatoes he saw a paper impaled on a stake which had been driven in with the blow of a shovel: IF YOU DON'T MIND YOUR RIGHTS I'LL HAVE THE LAW ON YOU.

It'll keep her thin, he said, riding up and down.

In the springtime when the water broke on the hill and the feed lots turned liquid and spilled the winter corruption into the creek the water was useless for anything but stock. In the summer it was an endless source of argument and in winter, when the frost came, holes had to be cut in the creek with an axe. Water slopping from the buckets froze on the feet as it fell, froze the pail to the trouser leg and the bail to the gloved hand. Even in the house the water froze when the fire burnt out.

Mr. Ellicot had finished speaking. What he had had to say was simple and direct. In the autumn at the time of the harvest it is the custom of all Christian people to gather together to give thanks to God for the treasure of the field. Man of himself can do nothing, he said. He is helpless and unprotected as the very worm. In a group or in society he can do much. But even in society, without the help of God he can do little. It is God who plants the seed and makes it grow, and if seed falls from the hand of man, or drops from the beak of a bird, or is carried in the wool of the sheep, these are but instruments of His divine providence. God does not need man; but man needs God. As for God, he said, in His dealings with His creatures He works in his own mysterious way.

Behold, he said, the lily of the field. It toils not, neither does it spin. But Solomon in all his glory was not arrayed as one of these.

That's certain, said Sam, as if he were following the straight path of Mr. Ellicot's argument. But his eyes were fastened on the pearl bobs in Mamie's ears.

———

Just after they had been married Mamie had taught Bill to dance the hesitation waltz. By custom they led off the dance. Myrtle Farish had been asked to play. Mr. Ellicot sat with Mockett on the chintz-covered chesterfield which had been pushed back against the wall. At the other end of the room the long table had been placed close against the wall of bookshelves.

Every mail day Mamie added to her library. Every mail day the *New York Times* book supplement came addressed to Mamie. Every week before the mail went out she made her choice and every week she learned more about Freud or Madame Blavatsky or the private lives of these and those – poets, kings, trollops.

On the table stood a basin of trifle. In the mornings Mockett made the sour-dough cakes. At noon Mockett ladled out stew or cut a joint, dished up potatoes and poured out gravy. For a party Mamie herself prepared the trifle – cake, custard, jam, sherry, angelica. Mockett had carried in the heavy bowl for her and the plates and she had arranged a few late flowers and polished forks and set the table herself.

Mamie and Bill were swooping and pausing, dipping and swerving. Nicholas Farish was talking to Sam's Gladys. He did not know when to hold his peace. Myrtle was sitting at the piano letting her hands bounce and run over the keys.

Nicholas Farish moved over to George.

We can't stay very long tonight, he said. We sent her out to that registered dog of Grimmet's and she's just had her pups. Three of the prettiest dogs in the whole country they're going to be. One goes to Grimmet for his fee. The Indians are all wild to have some of that big dog's get. Floss knows how to take care of herself but I like to be about. If Myrtle hadn't been so keen on meeting the new teacher, dynamite wouldn't have moved me tonight.

Mr. Ellicot moved over to the pair.

What are you going to call them, Farish? he asked. It was the first thing Adam did in Paradise, you'll remember. And Adam gave names to all the cattle, and to the fowls of the air, and to every beast of the field. . . .

Myrtle's like Eve, said Farish. She's been doing all the planning. She wants something to suit, something local but romantic, something the imagination can play with. She thinks she'll call them Chilco and Chezacut after the rivers up beyond.

It's a pity, said Mr. Ellicot, it's a great pity, Farish, that you're not keeping the three. There are three rivers, you know, the Chilco, the Chezacut, and the Whitewater.

FOUR

Rose conceded. Since the school party was to be
on neutral ground, since Sam paid the most taxes,
she would go. Her only other appearance in public
she had made some years before on election day. The legend
of her appearance still made conversation.

The inhabitants of the House were liberal to a man.
From the government flowed grace as one was taught that
grace flowed freely from the fountain and source of being.
The government assigned mail contracts and contracts for the
supplies that went to build the reservation flume. It was the
government that made the crooked paths straight. It paid
men for rolling away stones and for repairing culverts. Between
the government and the electors who lived scattered through
the inaccessible reaches of the rural riding the member was
mediator. And if the lot of man had not been predestined
since the beginning of all government, it was certainly determined contingently by the choice of the current member.

Mockett understood policy and politics and was never
happier than when he was engaged in official business. At election time there were a great many things to do. He lingered less

over his cow, neglected a column or two in the *Manchester Guardian*, was less curt with Mrs. Hawkins in the store, despite the fact that as an American citizen she could neither help to choose the mediator nor profit by his bounty. He spilled a good deal of ink and could be seen writing in the store under the flicker of a coal-oil lamp.

There was no doubt, to be sure, of the results of the vote. It was invariably the same. However, out of the spirit of festivity, which the occasion of an election seemed to warrant, Mockett had Bill's younger boy, Christopher, letter some posters in which the word Liberal was joined to the phrase One Hundred Per Cent.

On election day food was to be had at the expense of the House. Even old Bill Griswold, who lived six miles above the Porcupine when he was not doing for someone else, came to vote. Horses were tied to the fence by the store. Sam came with Reg in the morning and after they had voted stayed to chat with Bill and Mockett. Such fraternal gatherings were rare. By noon almost everyone who had a vote had marked his ballot.

In the latter part of the afternoon Rose appeared at the store. She had never been known to vote though her name always appeared on the list and it entered no one's head that she was about to exercise her electoral prerogative. Mockett with unusual alacrity placed himself behind the counter, hesitating between the place from which he weighed out flour and sugar and the wooden cage sacred to the performance of his duties as postmaster.

Well what can I do for you today, Rose? he said as if it was his usual custom to wait on her.

She looked at him and walked over to Mr. Thompson, who was the poll clerk.

Rose Flower, she said, housewife.

Mockett, left stranded behind the counter, went into the postal cage and started arranging stamps.

Rose disappeared behind the curtain. In a moment she emerged. Without looking at the group around the table she went to the door. At the door she turned towards one of the posters pinned up by Mockett.

Well, she said, so that all could hear – so it is, is it?

Then she made off.

Mockett scratched his head and looked toward the particular sign on which Christopher had written DEEP HOLLOW CREEK, ONE HUNDRED PER CENT LIBERAL.

Now, said Mockett – turning to Farish, who had been talking to Mr. Thompson – I wonder what's eating her.

Here in the cleft of the valley, Stella thought, it is difficult to distinguish comedy from tragedy. What is man alone in his cabin that he is fashioned so curiously and dreadfully? Call in the gopher to witness and the spider, the whisky-jack and the chicken hawk. Call in the reader of the *Western Monthly* to assess his two-gun heroism, his superhuman struggle in the grizzly's embrace.

To the school party came Rose, orange tam-o'-shanter defiant. To the school party came Mamie, carefully through the dust of the road, dress lifted, buckles glinting, bobs of oriental pearl, jacket collared with ermine, real ermine, soft ermine, caught by Bill in a spring trap. Came Bella, Reg's wife, sound of whip on flank, the old horse Aggie hastening a step, falling into an amble, into a doze. Came Myrtle Farish, though she had no children, poor little thing, only a dog, a brown curly coated vicious creature taught by Farish to insult, craftily taught to stay on the place, to eat only from his hand and Myrtle's, taught to stay just within the bounds of the law – no more.

It is a mercy they have no children, Mamie said to Stella, what that man would teach them.

Came Myrtle on sufferance, bringing sandwiches tied on behind the saddle.

Came Dick Mockett late, to stay only for a minute until things started, bringing a frosted cake all set about with silver beads and angelica.

No one has asked Mrs. Hawkins, thought Stella, no one has asked Mrs. Hawkins.

I say, said George – who was to be the horse in the play – I say look at the old hawk down by Uncle Bill's chickens. I'd plunk him if I had a shotgun.

You'd plunk him, George, tittered three little girls, jumping up and down.

You'd have to walk some first, said Gladys, seizing Ellen, one of the witches, adjusting the pointed cap pinning the black skirt.

Space was cleared in front of the room, desks shoved against the wall. Cora was standing on the table, looking over the partition.

Rose gazed straight ahead, body turned towards Bella five degrees. Mamie, vivacious, chatted with Myrtle Farish.

Mockett arranged it, she said. The registrar wrote to him. All changed now. Tables, you know. And such a business hauling them in. Real desks with glass inkwells, just like a city school.

Gladys bowed. Silence. Four pairs of eyes focused. In the lunch room there was a rattling of pans. From behind the partition came a groaning and murmuring.

Christopher told me, said Mamie.
It's George, said Rose.

(Enter Ellen, Cora, Anna, twisting and
shuffling)

Thrice the brinded cat has mew'd;
Thrice and once the porky whin'd;
Coyote cries, 'Tis time, 'tis time.

In the centre was Mrs. Reg Flower's dutch-oven, brought
by Aggie, adding to the weight up the hill from the river.

Round about the billy go,
In the poison'd fox bait throw;
Toad that under cold stone
Days and nights has thirty-one
Swelter'd venom sleeping got
Boil thou first i' the billy pot.

Double, double, toil and trouble,
Fire burn and billy bubble.

Fillet of a rattle snake
In the billy boil and bake
Wing of mallard
Food from Ballard
Three hairs from the house cat's tail
Clipping from the horse's nail

Double, double –

Anna:

> By the rattling of his spurs
> Something wicked this way whirs.

> (Enter Christopher)

> How now you spavin'd, bob-tailed nags
> What is't you do?

Ellen, Cora, Anna:

> A deed without a name.

Christopher:

> I conjur you by that which you profess
> How'er you come to know it, answer me:
> Though you untie the winds and let them fight
> Against the hay stacks; though the muddy Fraser
> Confound and swallow all prospectors up
> Though the range and rolling hills
> Do slope their heads to narrow Deep Creek,
> Though Russian Thistle and alfalfa mate together
> Answer me.

Mamie's ear-bobs turned towards Myrtle Farish.
Such a nice cake, she said. Angel-food. Mockett made it.
I put on the silver balls and the angelica.
Fox-bait, snapped Rose.

Ellen, Cora, Anna:

> McTurk, McTurk, McTurk, beware.

Christopher could have done the real thing you know, said Mamie, but George . . .

Christopher:
> Where is my strawberry roan?

Ellen, Cora, Anna, in wavering harmony:
> Out, out on the range
> Where the heifer and bull calf stray . . .

(Enter George)

It's real – real hair, explained Cora, the hair that Papa Sam cut for the dealer even if Christopher brought the blanket.

Exit George in the blanket, real horse-hair sweeping from paper head. Applause. From behind the partition came the sound of feet and voices. The pot, the blanket were put in the cupboard. Sandwiches and cake appeared.

Stella heard fragments of conversation.

Mockett says that if we hadn't written – it was Mamie's voice – he's a fine man, a fine man.

Very fine – it was Rose's voice now.

He is indeed. Twenty years I've lived with him – it was Mamie's voice edged like broken china. If any one knows Dick Mockett's worth . . .

So you admit it, said Rose, Mockett wearing the stones flat up to the Porcupine and the floor boards carrying the slop bucket. There's some – despite the tales they keep telling and telling of others . . .

Out through the door, back to the parlour and the lace curtains, back between fields mowed flat went Mamie.

Myrtle Farish poured out cocoa. Cora passed sandwiches. Christopher, gathering up his blanket out of the cupboard, went out the back door.

No, it would choke me, said Rose, looking at the fluted frosting and the angelica.

I told you, she said, turning to Stella, I told you to let well enough alone.

I'll drive you to the gate with Aggie, Rose, said Bella.

Let us put away the things, said Myrtle Farish.

Safe in the parlour, safe behind the lace curtains, Mamie wept – not stormily but quietly – dabbing her eyes with a lace-trimmed handkerchief.

Sam'll make her apologize, said Bill, if he has to put a rope on her to bring her here – the great she-moose – and you so little and defenceless. If he don't I'll take my gun to him. He'll bring her and he'll bring her quick and she can get down on her knees to you.

Called for by Mockett Stella stood there not to comment but to witness, not to speak but to be spoken to.

It was your place, said Bill, to bring the olive branch, not to come into a community causing disturbances. Living up on the hill you're on their side. She was let come all the way alone and fainted on the doorstep. You should of told off Sam's wife – you should – and you can tell her if she don't come I'll fetch her myself.

Let him come, said Rose, standing on the doorstep, look-ing down into the valley between the tangles of the vine stems which covered the wooden verandah. Let him come and Mockett too. And in the evening she climbed the hill behind the house to bring in a chicken which had built a nest in the brush.

FIVE

Myrtle farish had said, Come up for the weekend. You can try him out then.

Stella had decided to buy a horse. Sam had said that he would keep it in the stable with the other horses. He spoke of horses he had which he thought might do but he couldn't make up his mind to sell.

Besides, he said, they really belong to George. I give him the pick of the new colts for his year's wages. Mockett's poisoned him, talking of wages and man's rights. When George talked of going to the Rock to work I gave him some horses and his pick of the colts as they came.

One day at four Mockett had sent an Indian to the school. The man came with his dogs, a couple of thin-ribbed hounds. With him he led a dappled horse by a rawhide halter. Cora went in to Stella.

Uncle Dick has sent an Indian, she said, Old Saul John from Shallow Creek.

Stella went out.

The man said nothing.

Well, she said.

He jerked his hand towards the horse.

Gentle saddle horse, he said, resting his chin in the folds of cloth he wore knotted about his throat. Then he was silent again.

Stella stepped up to the horse.

No, he said, no touch.

I'd like to see him, Stella suggested.

Look, he said, no touch. Then, gaily, M'bee kick.

The horse stood patiently, its nose drooping almost to its broad and ragged feet. The long hair of its tail cut a monotonous semi-circle in the dust.

Fifteen dollars cheap, he said. Mockett say fifteen dollars cheap. You pay Mockett I leave the horse.

No, said Stella. No.

Day after day they came leading this, leading that — greys, pintos, sorrels — every bundle of bone and hair that could be led by a halter. The word had gone round.

Bill had horses but he kept only four in the stable, his own high-shouldered bay, Clarence's horse, and the team. If Mockett rode he rode one of the team — rode stiffly, slipped over the horse's back like a clothes-peg.

If you want a horse quite badly, George had said to Stella, I could put a rope on a fellow that runs out by the alkali lakes — Old Twister's colt, just coming three and ready to break. I'd tie his head down and clap a saddle on him and ride him about for a day or two.

But George didn't bring the colt then. It was only after Stella had left Sam's and was living in the cabin she had rented from Bill in the spring of the next year that George sold her a horse. George was eighteen then and had left school and worked all the time on his father's place. He went down to the store and sat with the men round the stove and heard Mockett talk to Hawkins's partner about freedom, equality, and the pursuit of happiness. No one paid much attention to Mockett and his talk of Tom Paine and others of his kind. It seemed doubtful whether Mockett paid much attention himself. George spoke from time to time but when he spoke the men did not listen to him. He had nothing to say that they didn't know already since he knew enough not to talk about Sam's affairs.

When Button, the horse which Stella finally bought from Farish, walked out to the end of the manure chute and dropped off into Bill's yard to his death, George brought the other horse down. It was a sand-coloured gelding – really a pony – and it walked with a quick strutting gait like a pigeon's. It twisted its head a great deal and mumbled its bit with its tongue. He asked twenty-five dollars for the horse and Stella paid it. He had told Sam what he was going to do because, despite Mockett's talk, he wasn't quite convinced that he had any rights at all.

Stella rode Pigeon for a day or two and kept him in Bill's barn in Button's old stall. He was touchy about the heels and moved his rump from side to side, blocking the way to his tie rope.

One evening George came down to the cabin. He sat on the bench rolling his spurs on the board floor.

He says to get him back, he said, putting some bills on the table. It's his horse and the price is thirty. He gave me the colt, he said, when it was a little long-legged gaffer. He gave it to me for wages. He said, If you stay with me you will have a big herd of horses and do better than them who work for the day.

That's easy enough, Stella said, take him another five.

But it's my horse, said George, and a sale's a sale. When a man does business he can't go back on what he's said and done. When a horse is sold a horse is sold. He said you've no legal right to make a bill of sale. Tell her thirty and I'll put my hand to it. He's broke his word, George said. It was my sweat got the colt off the range. I worked for him like he said.

In the end George took the money and left. The next day he came back with a bill signed by Sam:

One palomino fourteen hands branded C/4 on the left front shoulder. Sam'l Flower.

So it's a palomino, Stella said.

He said it's yellow like cream it must be a palomino, said George. There's no palomino stallion but if a colt come out yellow like that it should be writ down palomino.

That's not all, he said when he left, that's not all.

I had the leather for my own horse, he said, the next time he came.

He held a braided halter for Stella's inspection.

It takes a lot of careful cutting and oiling and plaiting until it's just right. You couldn't get it from Eaton's for five dollars, he said, not like this. It's work like the Indians do.

There are ways, he said, if a person sits down and thinks a little. There are ways which just about set a man right with things.

After Stella had decided that she might be able to buy her first horse from Farish, Myrtle had ridden down one Friday afternoon leading another of their horses so that Stella could ride back with her to the Porcupine. You can spend the weekend with us, Myrtle had said. Stella had packed a few things in a sack as she had seen others do and Myrtle tied it on behind the saddle.

When Stella had told Rose that she was going to be away for the weekend Rose had said nothing except You'll miss your bath.

Every Friday night Sam filled the tub in the kitchen from water heated on the stove. The rest of the family, as far as Stella could see, bathed in rotation earlier in the evening. The water offered to her was fresh out of the barrel. By the time she was called the children had been herded into the front of the house.

If you slip the latch on the door no one will bother you by chance, said Rose.

Stella hadn't thought of the bath when she accepted Myrtle's invitation.

It will save Mr. Flower bringing the water, she said.

He doesn't want to be saved, said Rose, not saved from that.

You will find it lonely at the Farishes, Mamie had said when Stella, who had come to pick up the mail, told her that she was going to the Porcupine for the weekend. They haven't anything, you know. I wouldn't ask you here, she said, because of Sam. Farish is not much good, she said. He spends too much time with the Indians. I wouldn't say a word against her, poor little thing. She likes coming here to play the piano and to borrow books.

Myrtle had said she would wait at Mamie's for Stella. She was a little afraid of Rose; she had heard so much she said.

She and Stella rode up the valley in the late afternoon. The autumn chill was making mists in the hollows and the leaves had been stripped from the cottonwoods.

It often snows in October, Myrtle said. Then it's too cold to get about.

Stella marvelled at the way she made the big horse she was riding walk.

Nicholas broke him, Myrtle said, no Indian jig for him.

Stella felt lost on the brown she was riding. The saddle embraced her back and front. The stirrups seemed to hang almost to the ground.

You'll get used to a western saddle, Myrtle said. Put your weight in your feet and forget about your knees. Sit tight in a lope and don't let Brownie jig. Walk along, Brownie.

Farish had supper ready when they arrived. He put the horses away in the barn and came up the rise to the house. The house at the Porcupine was built on a triangle of ground between the base of two hills. Part of the property lay on one side of the road. Part on the other. The creek was at the far edge of the second strip and from the distant bank of cliff rose ledge over ledge. When Stella looked from the door, she thought, living in the valley is like living in a pit.

Farish rolled potatoes out of the oven.

You can see the horse in the morning, he said. I don't know what you'll think of him but he's quiet and walks well. We can lend you a saddle until you pick one up somewhere.

The Porcupine seemed remote from the House. Blackness leant against the windows. They sat over coffee. Farish talked about his trapping days round Stewart, about the time he packed in the Kootenays, and of how he had met Myrtle, who was teaching in a school there. They had lived near Calgary for a while when he worked in the oil fields. They had stayed there as long as there was work. He had known the Indians about Calgary and had had some good horses in his day. He talked about the war – of how he had gone when he was seventeen and of how he had been taken prisoner and been sent to work in a mine.

We didn't work, he said. All we did was to plan how we could escape. We did one night. Three of us. And just as we crossed the border of Holland we turned back in a haze and walked right into the Germans' arms.

His life had been an endless fight against odds, Myrtle said. Her friends had told her not to marry him but she had known what she wanted.

Nicholas said he had known what he wanted too. Myrtle was small and plump and blue-eyed and had dimples in the back of her elbows.

She was trim and neat like a little Belgian mare, he said, and besides she knows more than most women. She painted that, he said, pointing to a picture on the wall.

Stella looked at the picture. The light of a forge lay red against a white background of snow. Snow lay on the roof and on the trees.

In a chest in the bedroom Myrtle said she had the blue satin dress she had worn when she was married seven years before.

When Nicholas went to the barn to water the horses she told Stella of how she had gone, the youngest girl from her class at normal school, simple as she was then, to the school near the lake over which she had to row each morning, and of how Nicholas had come every day on horseback until she said she would marry him.

With Nicholas from the barn came Flossie, the Chesapeake, two pups at her heels. Nicholas had thrown down hay and watered the horses for the night.

He was just putting some sticks into the air-tight heater when the outside darkness was silvered by a ray of light and the silence broken by the scraping of an engine and the sound of voices. Then up the steps they came – Mamie, Mockett, Bill, and the boys.

We couldn't be left out of things, said Mamie as she came in. How different it all looks, she said. When we lived here, she said, we had a carpet on the floor. We had a green carpet with pink roses on it. In winter when the snow blew against the door and I could see only the flatness of the white hill and nobody came, the carpet made me feel warm.

Farish was bringing a bench from the kitchen.

Have you got the cakes, Dickey? Mamie asked. We brought a party, she said, with us. We couldn't expect you to do for the crowd of us. Couldn't expect it when you have a guest. The men sat down but she kept moving about – looking.

I could let you have some chairs, you know, she said to Myrtle. Dick has ordered a new set for the outer parlour – such pretty ones too. We could get Griswold to bring up the old ones the next time he comes down with the team.

We have all the chairs we need, said Farish. We don't often entertain and those we do take us as they find us. Thank you just the same.

Farish wound the box gramophone.

Come on, Mrs. Flower, he said, we'll start the fun.

Round they went, Farish stepping and strutting, halting and chugging, breaking into a chicken scratch and then into a Charleston.

She won't miss a step, Stella thought.

Mockett was trotting Myrtle.

I usually dance, he said, only if the music is a waltz. He moved as if, after years behind the counter, he was warming up for a foot race.

The rest sat.

It didn't take you long, Farish, Mamie said, to get Sam's boarder up.

Myrtle asks whom she pleases to her own house, he answered.

About eleven o'clock Mamie suggested supper.

Since it's a surprise party, she said, we'll cut the cakes.

Myrtle took out cups. Farish made coffee.

Dick has coffee in the box, said Mamie, and a jar of thick cream. You haven't a cow have you, Mrs. Farish? We had a good milking jersey when we lived here. Now I don't know what possesses Sam, she said. He never keeps a proper cow. He just culls anything that's handy from the range. Rose can't have much cream. I knew when I first saw Sam that he'd never know how to live.

As the darkness closed behind the Flowers' leave-taking Farish shut the door and, leaning against the frame, looked at Myrtle.

By all that's merciful, he said, put the coffee pot back on the stove so that a man can drink a good black cup of coffee in his own home after pandemonium has been freighted out of the country. Now what could she want?

I suppose, said Myrtle, she didn't like to think of something going on that she didn't have a hand in. I suppose she didn't like to think of a party she hadn't made. It's nice being the centre of things.

In the morning Stella tried out the horse, Button. In the first place Stella disliked the name. Besides, Button was short and round-barrelled. He was not her idea of a saddle horse. Had she been writing her own bill of sale she would probably have written him down "chunk" and left it at that. Picking his way along in his number-naught shoes he reminded her of a deep-bosomed city matron. She would, she thought, have preferred something more virile. However, she felt desperate. At the moment a horse which she could ride when she chose stood for all the things implicit in Mockett's murmurings about freedom, equality, and the pursuit of happiness. With a horse she could come and go without depending on others.

That morning as Farish led the horse out of the barn she felt as she had felt the day before when she had ridden up with Myrtle. After she grew up she had learned to ride from an Englishman, who earned a fitful existence for himself, his wife, and his child by teaching whoever came to ride. At one time he had taught riding in a boys' school and he considered every decorum and nicety of the art. Had he taught classics or economics he could not have expounded the subject with more precision or exacted a more rigorous application from his pupils. Stella knew how to saddle and unsaddle a horse. His pupils began with the fundamentals and were taught the name and function of every strap and buckle. Before a man can operate a machine, he said, he must know the name and function of every part. Stella had been kept in the ring, putting the horse through every pace until she was fit for the road and the bridle path. She had learned patiently the name and function of every strap and buckle and now in her moment of need she was confronted with a confusion of straps and thongs and horse-hair bands and with a weight of leather which, she thought, I shall never be able to lift.

Sun was falling into the valley over the edge of the hills. There was no heat in it. Under the jack-pines along the bend of the road the shadows lay in dank pools.

———

Stella rode with Myrtle up to the canyon. Here the hills pressed together as if they wished to cut the valley off from the rest of the world.

We will be cut off soon, said Myrtle, as if in response to Stella's thought. When the snow falls it drifts into the gap. Only the water keeps flowing, under the ice. One can always get about on a saddle horse though, she said, if it's kept rough shod.

I couldn't shoe a horse, said Stella, I hadn't thought of that. Sam would do it, I suppose, but so much then for freedom and liberty.

A man is not an island unto himself, she thought, *There was a time when all the body's members. . . .* Poetry could rise to eloquence. One could fob off a fact with a line. The right eye scanned the testimony of the left and in the margin the hand wrote *lyrical self-pity*. The hand wrote *To be considered: Thoreau on the shore of his lake   Steffanson in the Arctic.*

Nicholas will shoe him for you, Myrtle said. Perhaps now that you know the way and have a horse you can come up on the weekends. It's lonesome here, she said, and it must be terribly noisy at Sam's with all the children.

SIX

Whaten Stella rode down early on Sunday afternoon because she had to see about settling the horse in Sam's barn, things seemed different.

Sam glanced at the horse with an appraising eye and commented briefly, I hope you didn't get done on the deal.

Secretly, too, Stella wondered. The horse seemed to move only with the utmost persuasion of heel and voice. Twice on the way down she had dismounted to see whether or not some of the straps and ties had worked under the stiff and flapping skirts of the saddle. The saddle seemed to need oil. The leather was difficult and refractory.

The days passed. The shadows lay longer under the pines. Sam rose at five in the dark and ground coffee in the cupboard. Then he and George and Gladys and the rest sat in the kitchen waiting for the light to break so that life could go on as usual. The cattle were beginning to stray down from the hill and Mockett talked of bringing in the rest of the carrots. Testing the air with his hand, he would say – There's a little growth in the ground yet. Every year the winter robbed him of the last fruits of his field. His procrastination was his mute recognition that when all was said and done nature still had the last word to say.

Then the men rounded up the cattle, branding with a great searing of flesh which seemed to float down into the valley like the smoke of sacrifice. The big branding was done in the spring but there were always the late calves and the strays that had been missed in the first count.

Bill looked over his sleigh, noting the slow approach of the time when the car could no longer haul the mail and freight from the Rock. It would take him four days, soon, two to go and two to come.

Mamie flicked the pages of the catalogues, thinking of Christmas.

The sponge, the bitter grey sponge of Rose's bread, was secured against the night chill by an extra blanket. The yeast worked sullenly, dully.

The next time Stella went to the Porcupine Rose made no comment at all. This time Stella came down early on Monday morning. It was the first week in November and during the night a light snow had fallen. Button's feet left gashes in the white web of it. Nothing was stirring on the road. Only the cattle in the feed-lots moved slowly about, pressing towards the great railed stacks.

The first snow was late. Sometimes it fell in October. From October to May life moved slowly in the veins, flowed under like the water pressed down in the creek under a lid of ice.

Stella beat her arms against her body as she had seen the men do. Button was covering the road with unusual alacrity. Stella had learned from Nicholas that horses broken by spur respond only to spur. She had objected on aesthetic grounds – on humanitarian grounds. However, here she sat, thrusting her feet a little forward in the stirrups, jingling a pair of wrought-iron spurs furnished by George.

Button hastened on, the breath rising in clouds from his nostrils, his tail switching slightly. He had grown accustomed to Sam's barn and moved towards it with unerring urgency.

The Flowers had already found reason to complain of him. On Friday Gladys had saddled him for Stella and as she pulled the cinch strap tight he had nipped her as she bent over to pull. He had bitten her gently but maliciously on the curve of her blue cotton overalls after she had winded him to bring down the swelling of his girth.

Gladys prided herself on her horsemanship, Stella knew. Caught between Rose's indifference, Sam's preoccupation, and the stream of suggestion from the House, she tried unsuccessfully to follow the middle way. At school she was a diligent pupil, learning without imagination whatever was to be learned. She could do the work of a man and helped Sam about the chores. She rarely spoke to her mother and seldom helped in the house.

When she had brought the horse round she had remarked, Farish doesn't know how to teach a horse stable manners. You better watch him. He nips.

Sam was still at the breakfast table when Stella went in. George had taken the horse as she rode up. It was part of the ritual as Gladys's saddling had been. Stella could keep a horse but she must stay out of the barn. The barn was sacred to Sam and Sam's. The objection Stella thought was sound enough.

Sam's face twitched and he brushed the curls back from his narrow forehead. Suddenly Stella wondered about his hair.

It seemed always the same length. She had seen Sam cutting George's hair and trimming the straight bobs of the little girls. He had shears and a pair of clippers that he kept on the shelf with the Sloan's liniment and the carbolic.

When's Farish going to send in his board bill? he asked abruptly. Four days here and three days there – you can figure that out at thirty-five dollars a month. You can't tell me he feeds you for nothing.

Stella hadn't thought of it, hadn't thought of Farish and Myrtle and the ten dollars a month going over the counter from the envelope to Mockett.

When I undertake to feed anything, said Sam, it's up to that something to be about at feeding time. Things belong in their own feed-lots not wandering about the country picking up hay from others' stacks.

You get your money at the first of every month, said Stella. You know when I'm going to be here and when I'm going to be away. No one has asked you to pay out anything or to give up anything.

Words tumbled on words – meaningless. Sam had had his way and had triumphed. Stella felt every fibre vibrating and the vibrations passing along the nerve, pricking behind the eye narrowed against self-exposure. Despite her anger she knew that Sam had placed her in a point of contempt. She had escaped one bondage to slip into another. She had accepted hospitality as thoughtlessly as the animals who seek shelter where they can find it.

When she came out of her room to which she had retreated, Sam had gone. Rose stood by the stove, fingering the handle of the granite coffee pot.

I told him not to say anything, she said. Whatever you say, I said, will be too much. He was down to the store yesterday to get some nails from Mockett. The order didn't come. Bill was sitting there by the stove and they got to talking. Whenever they get to talking something happens. Bill was still threatening Sam to bring me down on my knees to her to ask for pardon. But it's just talk and he knows it's just talk. Then Bill said to Sam that he was having a pretty hard time keeping his boarder here. He said Mr. Thompson never left the House. He said it's because you never should of took her in the first place. You've got nothing there but kids and cows – nothing at all to please a person's fancy.

Stella said nothing. There seemed nothing to say. It was then, though, that she decided to live by herself. As far as Rose was concerned she supposed it was rank desertion.

There is always one comfort, she thought, Rose knew it wouldn't last. In some strange ruminative way she has prepared herself for what I am going to do. Life breaks itself against her and the only peace she finds is in fingering the fragments.

Mockett, approached, was diffident.

Women don't do it in this country, he said. There's only one kind of woman lives alone and it's not for quiet's sake she does it.

The facts remained unaltered. Bill had a two-room cabin which had been at one time Mockett's house. When Bernard deserted Minnie, going off and leaving Sam to settle the wreckage of the taxi business, Mockett had remembered his promise to stand behind her when Bernard should fail. It was only in her disgrace that she would have had him and he knew it. She had been spoiled by everyone. After Bernard left, Pa sent her to the coast and when she came back freed apparently of the legal claim of Bernard, Mockett married her and took her to the cabin to live. The cabin was made of twelve-inch logs and Mockett had finished the walls inside with laminated board so that it resembled a low-weather tight box. It was built at the side of the field not far above the creek. Here they had lived. Then Minnie went. But he stayed on in the valley as if his marriage had never been. The whole creek smiled at the discomfort of his presumption, because Minnie had not been free at all, and when the final freedom came she went to live with a man who could give her more than Pa's clerk could. It was a pleasant jest to see Mockett, wise in law and legality, trumped by his own sentiment.

When Minnie left, Mockett moved back to his room in Pa's house and lived just as he had lived before. It never seemed to occur to him to try his luck somewhere else. At various times people had lived in the cabin but now it stood empty with a lard pail turned over the hole through which at other times the stove pipe had extended.

Bill had taken the cabin with the property. He debated. He talked it over with Mamie. He suggested obliquely that Stella change her boarding house. The cabin, however, seemed to be a neutral solution since Stella was determined not to understand his suggestion. He would write, he said, when she went out for Christmas. Nothing could be decided before then.

The snow began to fall. It drifted in piles against the barn. At the school Bill's boy Christopher lit the fire in the drum heater one week, George lit it the next. The children boiled cocoa in a pail.

The mail came in two days late. The snow was drifting on the mountain. It was almost too cold to ride. Stella had bought a pair of moose-hide moccasins at the store but she had nothing warm and loose enough to wear. The lacing in her winter riding breeches constricted her knees. At night she turned the pages of Rose's catalogue.

We'd better turn Button out, Sam said. He can come in from the yard at night with the others. It's too cold to ride about the country unless you have some determined purpose.

Stella sat at the school late, for peace. There was no lamp so that darkness set the limit of her stay and darkness came early.

One day there was a great howling on the road. Dismal and shrill the voice rose crying through the cold air. Stella went to the door. Two by two the horsemen came, Indians astride, three pairs of them in all, and behind them a sleigh drawn by a thin sorrel mare with a yearling colt running at her side. The wail rose as if to pierce the dove-grey sky, as if to level the tops of the hills.

Then Stella remembered. Up at the Rock old Susannah's boy had died. Surely it was Susannah sitting in the back of the sleigh behind the coffin, like it covered with a blanket. The cry rose as she beat her head on the blanket-covered boards, up and down, up and down.

George's words recurred to Stella. A dead body is an awful thing in this country now. Stella wondered what they would do when they got to the reservation. Behind the sleigh bearing the coffin came the dogs, great lean hounds yelping with the excitement of pursuit.

Stella had heard of old Susannah. She was a princess of the tribe, the band of Shuswaps known in the country as the Sugar-beet Indians. In the days when men had come to pan the creek for gold she had been courted and carried off to China by one of the smooth-faced Chinese who panned gold in the creek. All the way to China she had gone, straight from the rolling folding endless hills, from the cottonwood, from the jack-pine. She had slipped away in a stolen moment and had returned a year later no one knew how. She had been to China and she told haltingly of the wives who had attacked her as a wild beast is attacked. She told of long pink nails and flat half-lidded eyes and endless torment. She had been flayed as one flays a rabbit and plucked as a grouse is plucked, feather by feather. She had prayed to the gods of her fathers and to the man who had brought her to this shame. He had taken her back through the streets and she had come again over the lake rolling with great waves – a lake as wide as the whole country. She had been tagged as the strange men tagged deer. She had come she knew not how, and from time to time she remembered that she had been in the past in a land which no one else had seen.

When Christmas week arrived Stella drove up to the Rock with Bill in the mail sleigh. From there she would go down to the coast by train. She knew when she was going that she would come back. For, she thought, when spring has come I hope to see the resurrection of the dead. I came just as the circle of the sun contracted.

She had heard of spring on the hills and along the creek.

For the time being she had lost her bearings, she felt, and been engulfed in the vast rolling waves of the folding and unfolding earth.

She had supposed that she could measure out life with a school compass. The universe pinned flat on a drawing-board.

For two weeks now life would be centred again in the abstract point which had determined motion in the past. Once that past was present. But the present dies every minute, if it exists at all. It is and it is not. The mind preserves in amber the body of the bee. The honey, the comb itself, is wasted and spent.

When I go home, she thought, perhaps they will still be sitting by the fire and the shadow will be reflected from the shadow on the brass scuttle. The theme unaltered. *Dies Ira.* The mind has failed, failed with first-class honours, with second, failed in the departments of pure and applied science *cum laude.* I believe in the body, the creator of other bodies, and in the body's body conceived by the body, born of the body, and suffering under the body – the body crucified, the body dead, the body buried – the body rising in the grass and blossoming in the hedgerow. No ghost. No church. No communion except the communion of the body to protect the body against the body. The only ritual, the ritual of the horse, the mat, and the vaulting pole.

Bill drove the sleigh with the two horses up over the steep climb of the hill, then through drifts and across dead grass, blown, clear of snow, where the wind swept round corners.

At night they stopped at Napoleon Creek at the Alvarezes. They ate and Stella went to sleep in the priest's bed, the bed in which the priest slept when he came to say mass for the Indians. The bed was covered with a tufted white spread and the pillow sham was edged with a frill of starched lace. On the wall above the bed hung a crucifix and beside the bed lay a black bear-skin rug.

Old Alvarez was a Spaniard, who had come as a packer for the Hudson's Bay Company. His wife was brown and silent.

Bill and Stella arrived at dark and left at dawn and when they left, Mrs. Alvarez brought warm bricks and placed them in the sleigh beneath the hay which covered the floor.

Bill said nothing all the way. From time to time Stella got out and ran behind the sleigh to warm her feet after the warmth had gone out of the bricks.

When they got to the settlement at the Rock, Bill said – You can have the cabin. We decided you could. It'll be five a month for the cabin and five for boarding your horse. I'll get Mockett to tell Sam and we'll bring down your things. We'll put a bed in the cabin. There's a long table there we had when we used the place for a meat house last winter. You can bring in a stove and things from here when you come.

Stella thought she should tell Sam herself and decided to write from the hotel at the Rock while she waited for the train. The letter which came to her from Sam gave no indication that her note had reached him.

I thought you was a lady, wrote Sam. Now I knows you wasn't. I have more kids than anybody up the creek. I won't believe it though till I hear it from the mouth of your own lips.

Mockett had evidently broken the news as soon as the snow had drifted over Bill's sleigh tracks. Stella could see Sam sitting, pen in hand, the children sprawled about him at the table. Behind him stood Rose. Out of a September day Stella heard her speaking – I told him you can't hope to do it.

SEVEN

I n the cleft of the valley the snow was falling on the roof for which old Adam Flower had freighted shingles from the coast. Over the mountain road which led from the Rock the snow was drifting in swirls and eddies, deepening in the hollows, crust forming on crust. The flakes fell and the cold tightened. Then the flakes stopped falling and the blue weight of a clear sky lay on the valley as the ice lay on the creek.

You just made it in time, said Mockett, unhitching the horse as Bill brushed the frost from his eye-lashes, from the front of his hair, and from the scarf which twisted round his throat. It's not safe to go out at Christmas. You can't tell whether or not you'll ever make it back. Go on into the house where it's warm. We've been waiting for you.

Sam made a great circus, said Mamie, as they plunged from the arctic of the road into the tropic of lace clouds, paper lilies, and flower pied linoleum meadow under old Adam's tight-built roof.

Christmas had left its debris – paper garlands, a Christmas tree stripped, mocking the outside with its fleece of cotton-wool, its frost and hanging icicles, a tea-table set with a white cloth, the brown earth of the tiered cake showing darkly through the heaped snow of confectioner's sugar.

You brought your friend for company – for protection, Mamie half-asked, half-suggested, looking curiously at the tall girl who stood with Stella.

For social insurance, said Stella. But let me introduce her to you. Miriam Fairclough – Mrs. Flower.

Miriam smiled.

She had said to Stella, let me come with you for a month. I can learn to cook and I can take care of the cabin. I've always wanted to really live – close to something – the real sort of thing one reads about. I'll bake bread and bring water from the creek and wash things in a galvanized tub. One should of course have a baby in a snowdrift.

The tub had come and a black iron camp stove and an air-tight heater, packed in the back of the sleigh.

Mamie looked at Miriam intently.

A new ear to listen perhaps, Stella thought, a new cloth for the imagination to embroider with the swift steel of ceaseless chatter.

Miriam looked back.

She was tall and soft-limbed and, Stella thought, as translucent as a Limoges jar. Her great braids of red hair defied custom and her every movement seemed an affirmation of negation.

Mamie's eyes moved restlessly, waiting for the new ear alone, watching to see which turn the story should round, what perspectives should be revealed from the slope, which from the rock-ledge, which from the height, what gate should be closed here, what bars lowered there.

She suspects that impressions have been made already, Stella thought, the attitude already set.

Mamie chose the mode of open attack, the candid simple approach of direct inquiry. You know no doubt . . . You probably have been told. . . .

Myrtle and Nicholas Farish had come to Christmas dinner, she said. Nicholas had brought the sleigh and they had stayed the night.

If I were Myrtle, she said, I would be a little jealous. Wait until you see him in his concha-studded chaps. You will see him. He'll be down about the horse.

Dick Mockett, she said, could attend to the horse. There was almost nothing he couldn't do. He was, moreover, an eligible bachelor, or so to speak.

Stretched out in the lower guest room Stella asked herself why she had come back. The House seemed like a trap. She had thought they would move into the cabin the next day or the day after when the men had set up the stoves. Mockett had ordered wood from Saul Peter and the wood was stacked, he said, at the side of the cabin. There was no need to move quickly though, he said. Things had to be done. Perhaps it would be better even to wait until the weather was milder. The break had been made with Sam. Sam had raged and talked and threatened but he would not act. It might be more comfortable at the House especially since Stella had brought a friend who would enjoy the comfort, the company, the standard that Mamie set for living. Here was life as one read about it. She had, Mockett suggested, transplanted the delicate flower of culture into a barren soil. Yet here one could hardly note that the frail plant was rooted on rock.

She determined – he had said, addressing Miriam, softly pressing the tobacco into his pipe, looking at Mamie as she sat by the radio dialling and humming – she determined that she would never let the country beat her, and look what she's done.

In her sleep Stella thought she heard the children moving in the loft above her where Sam had put them to make room.

Under pressure from Stella, Mockett at last made the move to the cabin possible. He set up the stove, washed the blood off the long wooden table which had been used for a meat block, and had the dunnage bags and boxes moved from the store across the field.

Stella had brought some things with her. What she could buy she bought at the store – flour, sugar, tea, coal-oil. Mockett added some empty coal-oil cans and a wooden bucket which had been filled before Christmas with pink- and brown- and yellow-centred rock candy for the Indian trade.

I don't think you'll last here, he said, standing in the door, but you can always come across to live when you find out that women were not made by God to live alone in this country.

I know I am an anomaly here, Miriam said one morning to Stella, who was gathering together her papers and books. You so obviously are here earning your living in the way you have been trained to earn it. Rose? Mamie? What else could they do?

She lit a cigarette and poured another cup of coffee. Her braids fell to the waist of her green wool bathrobe.

I have an idea, she said, that if I really wanted to I could collect enough material here for a book. It's lying round everywhere.

Stella turned. The Arnold Bennett of the creek in the deep hollow? she asked.

The men, Miriam said, are the least interesting. But then I haven't met Hawkins' partner or Farish.

You have enough time to write if you want to, Stella said.

She put her pencils in her pocket.

You could ride up to the Buzzard on some pretext. I suppose Mrs. Hawkins' partner is not completely inaccessible.

The men I know, Miriam said, are so like their own golf sticks, so wrapped about with ticker tape. . . .

An anomaly here, Stella thought, as she pulled the door to behind her, an anomaly anywhere.

Miriam had already acquainted herself with the Indians. She had stopped once at the reserve to look them over. She had come back and returned to trade a yellow silk petticoat and a red knitted suit for a moose-hide jacket. The Indians, she said, imagining no other status for her, seeking a cause for her existence, had called her the school-lady's cook.

I told them, she said, that I had come to take care of you. It's rather a joke on both of us. But if it makes things easier why worry. I find it infinitely diverting.

In the jacket and a pair of green melton ski pants, a plaid scarf knotted round her head, she rode about the valley.

Bill and Mockett were good-natured, she said. Either or both of them helped her to saddle the horse. Mamie had called out one day to ask her where she was going. Only those who need or those who are demented ride for any reason at all, she had suggested.

She wants me to share her life, I think, Miriam had said. She wants me to sit and listen. But I want to see what I can. She amuses me. People amuse me, she said.

Since Miriam and Stella had only one horse to ride they rode singly. For the most part darkness closed in before Stella could go out. She saw no one but Miriam, who had taken over all the necessary business with the House. On her way home from school Stella walked quickly past the parlour windows and if

she took Button for a brief expedition she turned his nose up
the valley. At school Sam's children said nothing about the
change which had taken place during the holidays.

Miriam seemed to fill the cabin. Her papers were scattered on
the table. She sat knitting by the stove ready for talk.

Nothing disturbs her, Stella thought.

Miriam went to the store for supplies and to send the
weekly order to the Rock. She came back with bulletins from
Mockett. Bill and Mamie were sure the arrangements at the
cabin could not last. The break had been made with Sam and
the logical outcome was for the adventure to collapse and the
change-over made to living at the House. Obviously there was
no need to return to the hill.

One day when Miriam had gone over to get the mail there
was a tap at the door. Stella had heard the snow squeak as
an animal had rounded the corner. She thought it was
Mockett's cow which was turned into the field every day for
a little exercise. She was standing calf-deep in a coal-oil tin
of water, towels spread on the floor, water steaming in
another tin on the stove. She was enjoying the luxury of a
private bath. When she heard the tap on the door she seized
her clothing quickly – flannel shirt, frieze trousers, moose-
hide moccasins.

It was Sam. In his hand he had a paper bundle.

I thought, he said, I'd just drop in to see how you were
getting along. We've just killed and I've brought the heart.

He placed the bundle on the corner of the table.

You aren't tired of living like this yet? he asked.

Then his eye rested on the air-tight heater.

You'll freeze, he said. It's nothing but a flashlight. Bill ought to be ashamed of himself letting you get a thing like that. You'll have to put a quilt on it nights to keep it warm.

He shoved back the hair from his narrow forehead.

Well, I'll be pushing along. It's too cold to keep a horse standing on the lines.

When he reached the door he turned.

Rose'll be glad to see you any time, he said, and, going out, shut the door after himself.

Miriam came, her bag filled from the post. The stage had been in for an hour or more and Bill had brought back a bottle of rum from the Rock. He and Mockett had been having a nip in the store as they undid the freight.

I had to go to the House, Miriam said. They had gone over. I guess she's gone to bed for the winter now. Bill offered me some rum, she said. Mockett thought it would be nice to have a little party. Then Mamie said you'd be waiting for the mail so they went over to get it.

Miriam spilled the mail out of the flour sack onto the table and sat down, straddling the bench.

When the freight came in, she said, Mockett had been washing the linoleum in the parlour. He had left the bucket on the heater in front of the chesterfield when he went out. The big miner, Hans, who came in a week or so ago from the river, was with the others in the kitchen.

What do you think she can see in a man like that? she asked Stella.

I don't know, said Stella. You've had better opportunity to observe. Haven't you worked it out in your notes somewhere?

Miriam smiled.

I'd noticed him about, she said. But I never saw them in action before. He's a big awkward-looking German who was frozen out down on the flats.

However, she said, they were getting ready for lunch. One of Bill's boys – Clarence, I think – overturned a bench in the kitchen with an awful clatter. Mamie was standing just in the doorway.

I suppose she fainted, Stella said.

I don't know why she did, Miriam said. She was standing just in the doorway. As soon as the bench crashed she began to sway and fan her hands about. Mockett had just come in with my mail and was standing in the other doorway. His cheeks were pink and his hair was falling forward the way it does. Bill was just behind him, looking over his shoulder.

You must have been amused, said Stella.

Is there any little thing I could do, I asked her, Miriam said, like getting a glass of water. She paid no attention but kept fanning the air. Just then the big fellow came out behind her and down she went.

You won't believe what happened, she said. I wouldn't if I hadn't been there. Mockett dropped the mail and came straight across the room and grabbed her from Hans. Then he made for the chesterfield. Her feet in those little black pumps were stretched out almost rigid. Mockett's hair was in his eyes and the rum and cold must have done the rest because he walked towards the chesterfield as if the heater wasn't there. I heard Bill say something and just then Mamie's toe caught in the bail of the bucket Mockett had left on the heater. Mockett slipped in the water and brought Mamie down with him, seat first into the steam.

I suppose she came to, Stella said.

I never saw a better cure for a faint, Miriam went on. Then she began to abuse Mockett, and Bill took her part. She's my wife, he said, pushing Mockett aside, let me take her.

She looked at Stella and, picking up a pencil, made a note on the back of one of her own letters.

It must have been the feel of Bill's arms around her that sent her off again, she said. Now she's upstairs with Bill rubbing her wrists and Mockett wringing his hands. The whole house is in a uproar. I just picked up the mail and came away.

Miriam was right. The men paid heavily for the fracas. For over a month Mamie lay in bed and the men brought and fetched, and Mockett did more than his usual stint of chores about the house. For over a month the drama in the creek went on privately, or reasonably privately, within doors, and Stella and Miriam moved their own way with no more to trouble them than an occasional intrusive comment relayed to them from time to time.

Farish came down to shoe Button and stayed to supper. It was too cold for Myrtle to ride. She hadn't been very well, Farish said.

He's not at all what I thought he'd be like, said Miriam. He does a great deal for you, doesn't he?

The coming and going was noticed, and Mockett made an allusive jest the next time Miriam picked up the mail.

I paid a dividend on your policy, Miriam said. I said he could hardly have missed Farish since Button's shoes had to be heated in Bill's forge.

An anomaly anywhere, Stella thought. I can hear her breathing beside me but what do I really know.

Miriam kept on recording facts. Yet in her own way she seemed outside the life which stirred in the deep valley.

She watched, thought Stella, as a casual visitor to the club watches a game of tennis.

In the evening Miriam read *Moby Dick*, which she had borrowed from Mamie's shelves. Mamie had not read it.

There are too many damp, drizzly Novembers – cold, chilling Novembers – without reading about people who are afflicted spiritually with Novembers of the soul, she said.

Since I am living at a high altitude and a distance measured by miles from the sea, said Miriam, my imagination takes the swell of the ocean like a net. I would like to go to Prince Rupert or Skidegate or Cape St. James.

Every night she read a page. Then, putting the book down, she knitted on a yellow pullover and wrote endless letters.

No doubt, thought Stella, she is outlining the day's incidents with the flat precision of a pen tracing the contours of a microscopic section.

I have written, Miriam said, for things from the coast. I want to do some more trading when I am here.

I saw old Gabrielle the other day, she remarked. She had on the red knitted suit. It gave me quite a start. It was like an optical illusion. If she'd had a golf stick, said Miriam, I'd have sworn it was my aunt.

One day when Miriam was out riding, Aloyisha knocked. She came in and, sitting down, rolled tobacco into a cigarette.

The cook, she said, have green lace dress for him – patting the knotted flour sack she carried – moccasins for aunt. He send green lace dress from city. Aloyisha fly like jitz-wai.

She flapped her hands open and shut, mimicking the slow, precise gesture of a butterfly's wings.

Stella looked at the ice on the windows and at the rabbit fur of frost which was turning to liquid crystal on Aloyisha's old black sweater, at the cloth wrapped about her head and the sack tied with rope across her shoulders. She thought of the aunt unlacing golf shoes in an oil-heated bedroom, slipping feet into the soft embroidered hide of yearling buck. A tale to tell of a niece gone slumming in the wilds. Then she thought of Aloyisha floating in green lace through an endless summer of gold, which had been trapped like liquid in the trenches of the valley.

One day Miriam rode to the hill.

I don't know how it happened, she said. Things always seem to happen to me. There I was at the head of them, leading the procession down the ridge of the mountain.

I know, said Stella, George saw you. He's just left.

So I was seen, she said. I didn't see them coming. I didn't hear them following me. When I came to the bend on the other side of the cut-off I saw them – a whole file of them riding in the snow behind me. I didn't know what to do so I just rode on in front of them all the way down the mountain. And there was old Gabrielle in my aunt's red knitted suit, sacks wrapped round her legs and over her head, sitting in a sleigh with some others and a box wrapped in a blanket.

What did George say? she asked. No one here could ever have seen anything like it. It is a long way down the mountain, she said, and everyone in the valley can see the mountain road.

In the winter, said Stella, they die like flies.

The winter catches them, she said, as the sharp stake catches the deer when it jumps the crossing at the creek. The Indian gets the deer and the winter gets the Indian.

You sound almost like Farish, Miriam said.

I learn things from Farish, Stella said. He tells me things from time to time.

Look at the reserve, she said. The paradox is how anyone lives to grow old, to be an Aloyisha or a Gabrielle or a Saul Peter. I saw a mist rising in the valley, Annunciata told Farish. It came creeping on the ground to the door. Mockett gave me a charm in a bottle, a charm of oil, and I gave the baby the oil in a wooden spoon. Mockett is no Shaman. He is only hide and bones and thin grey hair against Coyote's mist.

The baby died, Stella went on, and they lit fires to drive away the mist and played lahalle as they will tonight.

Lahalle, she answered Miriam's question, with dice. Almost everything they own changes hands.

Where is the priest? asked Miriam. How can they bury a body without a priest.

EIGHT

Miriam stayed on. The tempo of the winter months was admirably adjusted to the slow rhythm of her pulse.

Farish came down on business, riding through to the range to look for a horse, calling at the store for mail and supplies. Then one day he brought Myrtle down in the sleigh to send her out with Bill to the Rock. She had pains in her hands and feet and red hard swellings on her legs and arms. Farish had wrapped her in a blanket and settled her in a nest of hay. He drove the sleigh slowly over the frozen road past Mrs. Hawkins' house. As they passed, he told Miriam, he had seen Mrs. Hawkins standing wrapped in a brown cloth coat, a sack over her head, looking up and down the road through a telescope.

She looked like Shackleton, he said, but all she saw was the sleigh and the team and me sitting on the box like a penguin on an ice floe. She couldn't see into the sleigh so she probably thought I was making off with a heifer's carcass. There's no limit to the mischief she'd think up.

He had sold a team of greys he'd managed to trade after the funeral at the reserve and was relieved that what he'd made would take Myrtle out to get the care she needed.

It's the country, he said, and the worry. She's been lonely since the ice locked us up.

Stella had not seen her. Miriam, who had never seen her before Farish stopped at the cabin, spoke of her as she laid the table for supper.

It's a hard life, she said, if you fight against it. As far as I'm concerned though I could live like this forever.

As Miriam reached up to move the lamp Stella noticed the curve of her hip under the gold-haired brown wool of her Harris tweed skirt and the light bathing her braided hair as water bathes pebbles in the creek.

Nor *in things extreme and scattering bright* – no *not in nothing* – certainly not in nothing. Why, Stella thought, slipping from the literacy of the past into the literacy of the present, must the immediacy of the moment act itself out in the klieg light of a thousand dead candles.

She rose quickly from the end of the camp cot on which she was sitting and, going to the bucket, poured a dipper of water into the white enamelled hand-basin.

Is supper ready? she asked.

Miriam felt the potatoes with a fork.

It will be, she said, in a little while.

All she does, Stella thought, is to get supper and take care of her own things and supper isn't ready when I come in tired and cold.

She sat down with elaborate carelessness and began to read. When Miriam put the potatoes on the table she read on, then placed the book open beside her plate.

Why don't you relax when you come in? Miriam asked. You poke round at the school all day and as soon as you come in you begin to read.

It's part of my life, said Stella. Just because I'm here there's no reason for letting my mind lose its colour like one of the cabbages in Mockett's root cellar.

Miriam unfolded her napkin and spooned potatoes and carrots from the green bowl.

I've made a new pilaf with the tinned meat, she said. It took me nearly all the time I had after Farish came in to warm up before he took the team back up the creek. He didn't like letting Myrtle go out alone but someone had to stay to feed Flossie and the horses. He could have turned them out, he said, but he hoped a week or two would put Myrtle on her feet again.

While Myrtle was away, Farish came more frequently to the centre. Sometimes when Stella came back from the schoolhouse she would find him chatting with Miriam over a cup of coffee. Whenever he came he cut a pile of wood and filled the box with kindling. They talked, apparently, about horses and the Indians. Farish, Miriam told Stella, admired her way with the Indians. They only do business with those they trust, he had said, and they only trust a real person. This, she felt, was a fine and subtle compliment. Among themselves, he said, they do not call you the school-lady's cook but ca-wa, friend.

Have you counted the moons since you have been here, he had asked her. The Indians say that the god Grisly Bear makes the seasons. There are as many months as there are feathers in the tail of the red flicker and as many moons in winter as there are feathers in the tail of the blue grouse.

Farish has a picturesque vocabulary, Miriam said one day.

You should become a contemporary Boswell, Stella remarked. You have enough opportunity to. You could turn your observation to account.

I don't know that I won't, said Miriam.

In the evenings Stella played a complicated game. She stayed up later and later so that she could sit alone at the long table after Miriam had gone to bed. Miriam slept late in the morning so Stella had to wait until unbroken silence or the failure of interest in letter-writing, knitting, or *Moby Dick* had sent Miriam to bed. Miriam too had a limitless capacity for reverie and a kindly interest in Stella's moods.

When Miriam finally went to bed in the next room Stella would sit listening to the logs crack with the frost, listening to the brittle scraping of the frozen bush branches against the logs outside. Once she heard a crying in the gulch out of which the old Hudson's Bay trail went over the hill. She thought it was a child lost and crying in the cold and she went to the door and stood until her eye-lashes froze against her face as she remembered that there were no children to cry. Only Lilac had children; the older ones were in the Mission school at the Rock and the baby would be safe in bed. Stella noticed the sky. It pressed down on the shoulders of the hills like an immense steel-blue mirror.

When the mirror is set up in the foyer, she thought. . . . Then she shut the door quickly as if dropping a curtain between the mirror and the reflected face.

From the gulch came the crying; but more immediately in her consciousness was the scratching of the bushes against the logs.

Then Miriam began to sit up later. She had begun to knit a skirt – a circular eternity of contemplative contentment, thought Stella.

January passed and part of February. Stella had told George of the bearskin rug she had seen at the Alvarezes'.

I didn't know, she said, that there were bears here.

George made no comment. A few days later, however, he came through the gate into the field on his fat white-faced horse. The horse shied at the gate, circling away from the rails and the wire loop which George was trying to slip over the post. It shook its flanks as if to loose itself from a burden. Swivelling on its forefeet it flung out its hind, lashing out and up.

What on earth is George doing? asked Miriam. I mean to the horse – and what has he tied on behind?

George had brought a bearskin. He modestly deposited the stiff hide which had been folded over into the semblance of a pack.

It didn't gall him at all, he said, as he ran his hand over the upper curve of the horse's rump. But they don't like the smell of bear – not any of them.

He looked at Stella and Miriam.

I didn't have two, he said apologetically, shifting the bundle with his toe so that it lay neutrally between them. I had it pinned up in a tree. Uncle Reg and I shot three-year-old cubs. He took his home. I didn't seem to have any use for mine so I pinned it up – out of the way of the coyotes – thinking I'd come back some time to get it.

He waited. Miriam smiled.

It's sort of nice black hair on the outside, he said, addressing her, and if you soak it in the creek in the spring you can work the hide. If I waited till spring, he said, you wouldn't get the use of it now.

He shifted the bundle with his toe a little towards Miriam.

You can put it by the bed to get out on, he said.

He stayed and drank coffee and talked about horses to Miriam.

I've got a herd of horses on the flats, he said, each and every one as good or better than anything Farish has. As for Bill and Mockett, he said, they don't know the tail of a horse from its forelock.

Stella wished he would go. She wished Miriam would go; she had long outstayed her invitation.

When Myrtle Farish came home Miriam went – not out of the valley but to the Farishes'.

I promised Nicholas, she said, that when Myrtle came back I would go up to take care of her for a while. I've only stayed here until she came in.

Then she packed her belongings and Mamie's copy of *Moby Dick* and went off with them in Farish's sleigh.

Thinking of Mamie's visit to the Porcupine, Stella said to Myrtle, It will be too cold for me to come up for a long time. I can't stand the feel of the stirrup iron at twenty below.

When Miriam had gone she moved about the cabin changing things to alter the look of the room. Then she went to bed and lying in bed she heard the bushes moving stiffly in the draught of air.

The next day Mockett knocked a little after seven. The thermometer was falling; there would be no school. Stella read most of the day. When the temperature slid under twenty below, Mockett had said, the school closed automatically. Even with a fire in the stove, the frame building was much too cold for the children. We didn't build a log house, he said, because we wanted the real thing. You couldn't paint logs neat and white like the cattle-shoots – and we'd set our mind on a white schoolhouse.

I'll come over with the reading tomorrow morning, Mockett said. Stella had never thought of buying a thermometer and it didn't enter Mockett's head to bring one.

When the school opened again in three days, Stella called at the House on her way back in the afternoon. She hardly troubled to think of an excuse for calling.

Stay for supper, Mamie said; young Mrs. Heppenstall is here. She adores horses too. She's English and she's married to the son old Mrs. Heppenstall sent to study at Oxford. When he'd done at Oxford he married her and brought her back to the ranch at Boulder Creek. I don't think his mother was very pleased with his coming back. From time to time she rides up through this cold to visit his cousins at the ranch – the Big Ranch, I mean. Why she should ride about in the winter I don't know. She is much too restless for a young married woman.

When Stella went into the inner parlour she saw what she had never seen before in Mamie's house – a real animal crouched in the corner of the room. Mamie laughed affectedly as a thin girl got up from the chesterfield.

If it wasn't Mrs. Heppenstall's, she said, of course it wouldn't be here.

She's nervous – the girl said, looking at the Labrador bitch – dreadfully nervous and she's used to being in the house now. The dogs I brought with me from England hate her, she explained, turning towards Stella. She was brought up in the barn at the ranch and I've seen her try to hide under the carpet as if she were trying to hide under the hay. Peter torments her and Paul treats her with contempt. Of course I've had them for years and she's new. Brian's uncle sent her down from the ranch. He thought Brian would need a good gun dog – but she's useless. She's afraid even of herself sometimes, I think. And the paradox is – the thin girl smiled fugitively – that her name is Juno.

At the sound of her name the dog began to quiver. Her hide twitched and rippled. She flattened her face on the floor and pressed her belly against the flowered linoleum. Her black nails ground into the smooth surface. Mamie looked at the linoleum over which the men were forbidden to walk in their heavy shoes – they changed to slippers in the old bar which now served as a bathroom and a stow-all.

After supper the Flowers played games to entertain their guest. Mrs. Heppenstall looked tired. She had ridden ten miles over snow-covered trails in the hard cold. The next day she would ride fifteen before she reached the ranch.

Mamie was enjoying herself. Mrs. Heppenstall's uncle-in-law was a man of some importance. Part of the time he lived at the ranch; part of the time he lived in what she thought must be luxury at the coast. He was a gentleman gentleman rancher.

The games, Mamie thought, showed her to advantage. Every game involved a feat of mental agility and mnemonic competency. The men sitting in their white shirts would play their parts. Only Mockett could triumph over Mamie but he never did. He knew how to gauge his failure to a fraction.

After supper Bill had been talking to Mrs. Heppenstall. They had been discussing a cure for side-bone.

Tut . . . tut, said Mamie, we have let you bring Juno in; surely we can leave the horses in the barn. Get the pencils, Bill, and the slips of paper so that we can all play a game together. Mrs. Heppenstall will beat us all – after all, Brian is a Rhodes Scholar.

Bill played intensely. Mamie looked at him from time to time – then at Juno shivering in the corner, her face pressed flat against the floor. They went through the alphabet, classifying novelists, scientists, patriarchs, prophets.

N, said Mamie.

Mrs. Heppenstall, Stella noticed, was moving her hands back and forth against the edge of the table. Mamie glanced at the various score cards. She had a comfortable margin.

Nations mentioned in the Bible, she said.

In a moment Mrs. Heppenstall got up.

Excuse me, she said, but I must bed down my horse.

The men have seen to the horses, Mamie said with restraint.

I always see to my own horse, Mrs. Heppenstall said.

Mockett got a lantern.

No, no – she stayed him as he started out the door with her – I always go alone. And he stepped back as she took the lantern from him and went out into the dark.

The fool, said Mamie, when the door closed. She might be kicked to death by a strange horse. If it wasn't for her uncle, Jim Fairbairn, I wouldn't put up with this in my house.

She rose and tickled Juno with the toe of her black pump. The dog shook. Then her lips curled back over her white teeth and with a quick gesture her mouth closed over Mamie's toe. Mamie was too frightened by what she herself had done to say anything. Juno had held her foot only for a moment – deftly and gently as she should have held the duck she might have carried to Brian's waiting hand.

Lord, said Mockett – staring at Bill's paper, which he had picked up from the table to divert attention – are there people called the Nasturtiumites?

If there aren't, Bill retorted, I defy anyone to prove me wrong. Even if there aren't there might have been.

In a few minutes Mrs. Heppenstall came in. She smelled of the barn, Mamie said the next day – and the whole house of vicious dog.

The next day was Saturday. Mrs. Heppenstall had said, turning to Stella, If you'd like to ride up the hill I would like the company.

What a fine-limbed dog Juno is, said Stella, as they rode up the slippery trail under the frost-plated jack-pines.

Do you like her? asked Mrs. Heppenstall. If you really do, you can have her when I come back. I'll ask Uncle Jim first. She's utterly miserable, she said.

A week later she rode down through the valley again. This time she did not stop at the House. Stella knew she had been because there were horse tracks and foot marks about the cabin and a pile of partly frozen dung. When she opened the door a dark shadow slipped past her.

Juno, she called, but the dog had disappeared into the bushes skirting the creek.

She'll go right back to Boulder Creek, Stella thought. She saddled Button and rode over the hill looking for the bitch's tracks in the snow. Besides Mrs. Heppenstall's tracks she saw only the triangular markings of a mule deer in the snow and the thin etching of a blue grouse's claws leading out from under a tree to a patch of torn snow, marked on either side by the knife thrust of a hawk's wings. A moment later she saw the body of the grouse. Mrs. Heppenstall's tracks were like fresh raw cuts in the road.

She must have ridden quickly, thought Stella, the hoof marks are cut deep. I wonder, she thought, why she left Juno.

After riding for half an hour she turned back. How could one overtake a dog in a wilderness of snow? Sitting at the table alone as she had wished, she quoted Goethe to herself out of

Matthew Arnold and she felt infinitely sad – in our life here above ground, we have, properly speaking, to enact hell.

Later as she lay listening to the scratching of the bushes, she heard another scratching at the base of the door.

It was Juno. She had snow between the clefts in her paws and lumps of snow frozen to her belly. When Stella opened the door she came in – erect on unbent legs. She ate what was given to her and lay on the rug near the bed.

And until Stella left – and after – Juno did not attempt to leave her.

NINE

Stella began to think of the spring. Winter persisted. The sweeping rhythm of the water could be seen only when the axe had cut a hole in the thick ice crust. On the ice-surface of the valley life moved severed from its roots.

Only by dissection, thought Stella, cutting the ice back from the edges of the hole – only by hacking and cutting can I look down into the moving centre. And when I look all I see is the moving water which will dry up in the summer heat.

She remembered sitting on the hill in the autumn looking down to Rose's folded land on the other side of the river. She remembered climbing to the ridge high above the road, which circled the shoulder of the hill like an arm in one of Blake's engravings. There she had watched a hill of ants – pulsing, moving, animate dust. Somewhere behind her there had been a movement in the yellowed grass. All about then was life moving unconcerned. The grass too must have lived. She had taken strands of it – flat and dry blades – and slit them lengthwise with her nail. Once there must have been sap, she thought, pondering the paradox of Rose's eyes.

In spring she hoped to see the young grass rise again from its roots, and the water breaking on the hill tumble over the ledge into the valley. On the hills calves would be dropped and in the grey shadow of the pine the slit yellow throat of the blue grouse would expand and contract with the booming exultation of courtship.

While the snow still clung to the earth Peter Paul's son was born. Peter Paul had a daughter already and a step-daughter, Felicitas. His wife, Felicitas's mother, had died in the heat of the summer before Stella came to the creek.

Felicitas kept house for Peter Paul and cared for her mother's child which lived tenaciously – persistently – through the cold winter months. Felicitas, who was twelve or fifteen years old, had assumed her mother's duties. She had cared for the baby, wrapping it in what cloth she could find. She had cooked the deer meat which Peter Paul had brought to the cabin in the corner of the reserve. She had scraped the hair from the skins of the deer and worked them as she had seen her mother do. And at night she had slept in her mother's place in Peter Paul's bed. If the baby cried she rose to hush it and what Peter Paul wanted she gave him simply without murmur as her mother had always done.

When Felicitas's baby was born Peter Paul was filled with pride. Stopping Farish on the road he said gaily, spreading his hands, I have done what you could not do; I have made a man. I will take Fleesa to the priest and I will call the man-baby Paul Saul. Then he rode to the store with Farish and bought a bag of flour and some mosquito netting.

The cold was relaxing. Here and there brown earth showed in streaks through the tattered snow. Sleighs travelled uneasily over the patched ice of the road.

One morning Stella saw them. The priest had come, she knew. Lilac, who had walked down through the cold to do the washing every week since Miriam had gone up to the Farishes', had sent Tony Bill to collect her wages, which she had asked Stella to send to Eaton's for stockings for the baby. He had come when the light was fading into darkness, tapping at the door, asking gruffly for the money.

The father has come, he said.

As Stella stood at the gate she saw them pass – Peter Paul driving the sleigh, Felicitas holding the children, the dogs following behind the runners crowding for place. Over her head Felicitas had wound the netting which Peter Paul had bought from Mockett. The frayed ends of the cloth fell over her shoulders and flowed out behind like a grey mist.

Mamie, standing in the window, watched them go too. Then she called the Catholic priest, Father Christopher, from his breakfast in the kitchen. At last he had come down from the Rock to inspect his flock.

You will have a marriage today, she said. Peter Paul is driving Felicitas to the church at Dedman Creek. He will be there before you.

She spoke of Felicitas, who had worked for her while the old mother still lived, and of Peter Paul's visit to the store.

Poor child, she said, she must scarcely have had strength to support the weight of it.

That night Peter Paul drove his family back to the reserve, the sleigh runners groaning and creaking. The next day they returned to Dedman Creek.

Father Christopher had spoken to Peter Paul.

I told him, he remarked, as he drank coffee in the parlour, that he must come back tomorrow. Then I called the

Rock. The law must be observed. I could not marry them. Some time the lesson must be learned. There are temporal punishments as well as spiritual. Of the spiritual such men know little.

Peter Paul waited the next day patiently. The Indian officer had made a quick trip so that he arrived in the afternoon with Father Christopher.

I am waiting with the money, Peter Paul said, to make things right for the man-baby. Ten dollars, he said, taking the money from a deer-skin pouch. I made him in the night without the priest.

It's the only thing he could have done, said Mockett to Stella, who asked him about Felicitas when she met him in the evening coming with his pail out of the barn. Father Christopher called the police. They have taken Peter Paul to the Rock. When the women are older it is a matter of adjustment. The men pay for the goods after they are consumed. Sometimes they never marry. If Peter Paul had stayed at home nothing would have happened. It was his pride and his ignorance. A minor is a minor, Mockett said. Old Father Christopher had to do it. Two wrongs don't make a right whatever algebra has to say about it.

It was not Peter Paul's taunt which brought a child into Farish's household. It is doubtful whether or not Farish ever consciously remembered Peter Paul's boast. Some weeks after Peter Paul had been taken to the Rock, and Felicitas and the children had been sent to the reserve at Dog Lake, Farish rode out with a team he had broken. He took the team to Lone Hill Creek to the game-warden. At the same time he took Juno to have her bred. It was almost as if Farish had arranged to assist nature – and fate had furnished Clintock with a need and an answer to Juno's need at the same time.

Clintock has the only male Labrador in the district apart from those at the Ranch, Farish had said to Stella. It's what Juno needs. If a bitch isn't bred she's nervy and timid. Take the deer now, he said, and the pheasant. The law's all wrong. When the bucks are thinned out and the cocks, the does get to fighting and the hens go round breaking up the nests of fertile eggs. Take Flossie, he said, she's natural and good-tempered. It's what Juno needs.

He came back in a week without the team and returned Juno to the cabin.

If all goes well, he said, she'll have pups in short order. I'll come down to get her a few days before she's due and we can take care of it for you.

He spoke of Miriam's visit and of the comfort it was to Myrtle to have someone with her while he went about the country trading.

It leaves me freer, he said, and Miriam seems to enjoy sitting about. She's a saddle horse whenever she wants and she's been mending and knitting and writing letters.

There was still snow in the valley when the water broke on the hill. Every day Stella watched the heaped rocks over which Mockett said the water would come.

Perhaps the thaw will come when I am asleep, she thought, or while I am busy about other things. I might go to the creek for a bucket of water and find that I have missed the moment of resurrection. I might sit reading while the fountain gushed from the frozen bones of the hills.

She was actually standing in the road by the store when Mockett cried out.

See, he said, it is coming. See the water slipping down over the rocks. Soon the feed yards will be a puddle of mud and we will have to haul water from the spring.

The day the water broke, Farish brought Miriam out. Myrtle's getting a child, she said to Stella as they ate supper, and I don't care to share the spotlight. I intend to stay with you for a day or two and go out with Bill when he takes the stage. Nicholas is going to the lower station with the team to pick the youngster up.

She patted Juno on the head and held the glass of cointreau which Stella had poured for her up to the light.

I've had it since Christmas, Stella said, but there never seemed to be any particular occasion for festivity until today. The water broke on the hill, she said, and I found a thick pink shoot of rhubarb in Mockett's old garden.

Miriam spoke about the child the Farishes were expecting. It's her brother's child, she said, but they can't adopt it, obviously. They've no visible means of support. I don't know the details but Myrtle thinks she can give it a better life than it's had. From all accounts that would not be difficult. Myrtle's made up the camp cot and she could hardly wait to paste pictures of dogs and horses on the walls – knee-high, you know – they see things from a different angle.

Farish came back at night with the child. He didn't stop at the centre. At the end of the week after Miriam had left with Bill on the first trip which the car made out Myrtle sent a note to Stella by old Griswold.

Since I can't get away, she wrote, come up and see us if you can on the weekend. If you ride up Saturday morning Nicholas will bring you down on Saturday night.

It's time I took Juno anyway, said Stella.

Every afternoon Juno waited for Stella at the gate. First she had showed black against the snow. Then the snow had bared the brown of last year's death and through the brown the green of the new life sprang and unfolded. As Stella came down the road past the House she could see Juno waiting at the gate of the field. They would go back to the cabin together and in the evening Juno would sit by Stella's chair while Stella ate and smoked and drank coffee and read late at the long wooden table. Sometimes Stella read passages aloud. She was completely aware of Juno's brute indifference but she liked to hear the sound of a voice – to hear the room filled with the exultation of a resounding phrase, or the sighing echo of man's protesting misery. The logic of discourse she reserved for silent meditation.

If I hadn't come here, she said, I doubt whether I should ever have seen through the shroud of printers' ink, through to the embalmed essence. The word is a flame burning in a dark glass.

For several days before Stella rode up to the Farishes Juno was not in sight when she came home in the afternoon, but as she opened the gate now Juno came across the field, walking quickly, like a woman who feels that despite the pressure of time her dignity is at stake. In the evening too she looked at the closed door and from time to time scratched to be let out.

The trip up the valley was like a pilgrimage. Juno went slowly. Stella thought of her burden and slackened Button's pace. At the turn before the Buzzard, Juno turned as if to go back. Stella urged her on. She often talked to the animals now. After hours by herself she felt the need to talk as she felt other primitive and essential desires. She would have waged battle in defence of the idea which she had come to hold with mute intensity – that man was beyond all else *animal loquens*. And, if the word had become for her the shroud, the thought had become the vital essence which could find realization only in the word. So Mamie talked, so Miriam wrote endless letters, and Rose lived only in the scattered moment of self-revelation.

Juno hesitated at the bend of the road, moved diagonally towards the irrigation ditch from which the sprouting grass had not yet been burned.

Oh no, said Stella. Remember. Nature's game must be played to the finish now. But you have the best of me. Not in one of the days of my years have I produced a single thing. I have grown by a force set in motion by an urge extrinsic to myself. I have grown like a plant and leafed after my kind – but here is the end. I live – she said, looking at Juno – like a stone.

Her words kept time to the swinging motion of Button's pace. She had, she thought, relieved herself and had straightened, by the mere sound of her voice, the diagonal bent in Juno's progress along the road.

In the meadow by the creek the sainfoin and alfalfa thrust and thickened. She lifted her eyes to the hills, which were brown and naked in the morning light.

Myrtle met her some yards from the Porcupine. She was walking and in her arms she had the child.

Unless I make a sling for him, she said, I won't be able to ride for some time. Imagine Nicholas bringing him in all the way from the lower station.

I'm going to break a colt for him, Nicholas said, when they met him at the barn. Children should learn how to manage animals themselves.

He had been cleaning out the barn and he sat on the door-sill with Flossie between his knees.

Stella spent the day with them and at night Nicholas locked Juno in the barn and rode down to the cabin with her.

We'd ask you to stay, he said, but the second bed's in use. I've made a safe place for Juno in the barn, you won't have to worry.

The darkness covered them like a quilt. The sound of Farish's breathing filled the space between the close, pressing hills.

There's something comfortable about a purple quilt, thought Stella, opening her eyes against the darkness, resting slack on the swaying darkness, giving Button his head, letting her hand lie ungloved on the coarse mane just above his shoulder.

Myrtle's never been happier, Farish said. I hope we can keep the child. Her brother's determined that his wife won't get it back. After all she's hardly a fit person to have him. Wallace doesn't think she'll find him with us.

Farish lit the fire for her before he took Button to the barn and while he put him in Stella made coffee. Nicholas will be back from the barn, she thought, looking at the domestic loaf and feeling the domestic warmth of the fire.

When Farish came back from the barn he drank the coffee and ate the sandwich she had made for him and talked about the pups Juno would have. After he had gone Stella sat reading.

The next morning she was reading again when Farish knocked on the door. When she opened the door he looked past her into the room.

Is she here? he asked.

Who? Stella queried, turning as if to call Miriam.

Juno, he said. She's gone. I've looked everywhere. She must have got out when I put my horse in last night. If she's not here the Indians must have caught her when she came through the reserve. They'll keep her until after she's had her pups. Then they'll let her go. They're crazy to get their hands on the pups of dogs like Floss and Juno.

For two days Stella hunted for Juno. She remembered that she had left Juno's collar on so that Farish could tie her if he needed to, and she thought of Juno caught somewhere in the bush. She remembered the time in the fall when a living branch had run through her stirrup. She had managed to press Button back until her foot was free but she had thought at the time of the raisins and hairs and tiles which had killed princes and philosophers – so swiftly does the soul escape from its uncomfortable casket.

Only the blood flows away, she thought, or the collar chokes off the furnace draught.

Farish came down again in the evening. He felt that he had failed in his trust. He felt even more keenly, however, that he had failed simply in the only business which he under-stood. The anxiety to escape blame and the anxiety to refrain from assigning blame drew the two of them for a moment into an understanding which Stella refused to recognize. She felt in his remorse an element of pity which her disembodied mind rejected. There was, she knew, something ludicrous in Farish's remorse which reflected her own inability to surmount the role of a vicarious Niobe.

Two days later Juno came back. In the dawn light she glowed black against the thick green of the rhubarb leaves which had unfolded from the fat pink shoots. She stood in the doorway uncertain, though she had scratched to be let in. She was thin and flat-ribbed again. After she had eaten she moved about the room and when Stella opened the door to get wood from the pile she disappeared. Then she came back only at intervals to get food. She must have her pups somewhere, Stella thought.

Close to the creek, under the log pig-pen which Bill had built after Mockett had left the cabin and he had taken over the property, Stella found her hiding place. But she saw the pups only when Bill and Mockett had raised the pen with a jack after Farish had failed to crawl in by one of the various tunnels which led to the nest. Under the pen Juno had dug a round pit and lined it with leaves and dead grass. In the hollow there were four pups, their bare pink bellies alone distinguishing them from the darkness in which they lay.

One of them was dead. Farish went to the cabin for a spade.

Well, said Mockett, wiping his hands on the sack in which he had brought the jack.

They'll go miles, said Bill, back to the place they know. She must have worked on the nest for weeks.

Farish buried the pup in the soft ground near the creek and covered the spot with stones from the creek-bed.

Later that spring, when Stella heard that Wallace's wife had started legal proceedings to regain the child, she remembered that Farish had said nothing. When the child had been taken away Farish packed the box in which Myrtle kept her dress and, with his saddles and equipment in the wagon, they'd driven out of the valley. Then the Porcupine stood empty again.

Stella went to see Rose one day after they had gone. Rose was emptying water from the bread pan into the flume when she rode up to the door.

There's nothing at the Porcupine, Rose said, but hills. I miss seeing Farish. He'd still drop in though he didn't come so much after you'd moved to the cabin.

But before the child was taken and the Farishes had packed up and left the valley they did Stella some service.

TEN

There is a courage deep-rooted in fear – the fear of being thought less able in body than those who live by the body.

The doctrine of equality, thought Stella, is rooted in unchristian pride and in unchristian fear. The weak pray for strength not to bear their infirmity but to cancel it – not to conquer their pride but to be equal to it.

That spring, before the Farishes left, and not long after Miriam had gone, she had fallen off her new horse Pigeon with a nasty thud when she had tried like the men to mount him bareback as soon as she and the horse came out of Bill's barn. Clarence, who was working in the yard, leaned on his pitchfork to enjoy the fun. Mockett, peering round the rump of the cow he was milking, chuckled. The cow switched her tail and lowered her head. He moved the tin pail forward and gave the cow a pat on the flank so that he could have free vision.

You better watch that bronc of yours, said Bill, leaning over the fence pole.

She had left the saddle at the cabin and she had either to jump on the horse as it stood or lead it across the field by the halter rope. Bill could have done either indifferently. Mockett would have led the horse without shame. Stella had fallen into Farish's way of speaking of horses as if she had been born in the saddle. Left to herself she would have turned the horse against a convenient bank, or down hill, or climbed on from the second rail of the nearest fence.

The men's glances determined her. As she swung herself up, the horse jumped forward and she found herself clutching for the mane on the side opposite her leg. Even in the minute itself she contemplated the ridiculous tableau – the centaur inverted – Icarus under instead of above the earth. Then her muscles relaxed and she fell, knees and hands in the dust, across the tongue of a wagon which had been left in the yard. Mockett abandoned his cow and came over to the fence.

Stella looked at him and laughed. Then, seizing the halter rope, she made off across the field. She was shaking and faint but she rode as she usually did at this time up the old Hudson's Bay trail.

From behind the lace curtains in the public parlour Mamie watched her go.

The next morning, as she bathed in the coal-oil tin, she noticed that her side was bruised and swollen. For two days she watched the faces of the children drifting before her on a wave of mist.

Slow, slow, fresh font, keep time with my salt tears. . . . In the afternoon she listened to the children recite their poetry.

How like Rose Cora is, she thought.

Standing on one foot, her hair hanging over her eyes, Cora stumbled through her lines:

O follow, leaping blood,
The season's lure!

O heart, look down and up
Serene, secure,
Warm as the crocus cup,
Like snowdrops, pure!

I don't think she really knows, said Gladys, what cro-
cuses and snowdrops are.

On the afternoon of the second day she decided to go
to the Farishes'.

I think you've broken a rib, Farish said. He strapped her
side to ease the pain and Myrtle urged her to stay.

We can take the baby in with us, she said.

It was still several days before the Easter holidays. Stella
was determined to go back. She didn't care to tell Mockett
and Mamie and Bill what had happened to her. She left the
Porcupine before dark.

I want to go alone, she said to Nicholas. Don't ask me why.

Pigeon moved along at his own pace. At the edge of the
road two young range bulls, which had wandered off the hills,
were throwing up dust, their foreheads butting into the crumbling bank. From the safety of Pigeon's back Stella looked at
them with respectful disdain.

Here was strength, she thought, sheer physical strength.

One of the bulls battered against the bank, dust spray-
ing like a halo round his dehorned head. The other looked out
from under a bang of rank hair suspiciously at the yellow
gelding picking his way through the dust of the road, turning
off to the opposite bank at the mere pressure of a pair of
cotton-clad knees.

Stella rode on. There were several miles yet between her
and the cabin. She no longer wished to speak aloud. She did
not want to hear her own thoughts. Spoken they would become

living things – fugitive – slipping away between the curves of the hills. She might meet them at the cabin – familiar faces with alien eyes. Mute like Rose, she looked impassively down at the arch of Pigeon's neck.

The world is my horse, she thought, and can be easily bridled. Slip the bit into the mouth with a little pressure at the sides of the lips. Hold the bridle so. Adjust the chin-strap with one hand, slipping the head-stall over the ears with the other.

The head of a horse is admirably designed for the bridle – she still looked down at Pigeon's head – ears to keep it from slipping, fleshy lip falling away from the straight line of the jaw, perfect adjustment to neat strapping. Try to bridle a frog or a snake.

I could bridle a bull if I dared, she thought, but better a gelding. Take off the young bull's horns. Turn him loose on the range. Let him increase and multiply and fill the valley with his kind – male and female – and when the fire burns out let him be brought into the valley, into the pasture, where as a bull-calf he kicked his heels. Let him be driven down the wind-parched road with the dogs and horses at his heels – down, down – then up through the white gates of the cattle chute.

She looked down at Pigeon.

All things have their use and predetermined end – the flash of a gelding knife – a spade has been set against the course of nature's Nile.

Strangely enough the bulls didn't look particularly happy in their strength and virility. Perhaps the memory of the winter feed-lot had lured them back from the still thin grass on the hills. They lacked manliness. They wished to lounge in the feed-lot, mouths agape, waiting for the hay which Bill tossed down from the wagon.

Pigeon picked his way along.

He had his compensation – a dry barn, a tin full of oats. He had had his troubles as a colt on the range but now he was pensioned into comfort – unless, like Button, driven by a desire which the knife could not touch, he walked to a fall in some wayward moment of self-assertion. He had suffered in the course of nature but he had gained from the point of view of solid comfort. There were others; true, less fortunate – Xavier's bay gelding scarred until the spur could do no more, lying out under the stars, finding comfort in a pile of warm manure.

It was as some men had maintained – and usually out of season – impossible to spy into the works of nature. Who knew what nature was? In the circus Truth sat in a tub, chin-deep, and the reflection meeting the face mocked its reality.

Some time before Button, quitting the warm contentment of his stall, had walked out to the end of the high manure chute and jumped into the yard, Bill from the rostrum of the haystack had delivered himself of weighty comment.

It is not natural, he said, waxing metaphysical and looking at Stella, since those who live by the mind sting pride in those who live by the body. It is not natural, he said, directing his irony against the roached mane of Button, who came at that moment round the corner of the barn. It is not natural to cut a horse's mane and pluck its tail. Why for did God give a horse a mane? To keep the heat offen his neck. Why for did God give a horse a tail?

His question had an urgency that was more than rhetorical. It dared the world to answer in words that could contradict the plain fact.

Mockett, who had been sitting on his milk pail, turning the pages of the *Manchester Guardian*, which had just come in the post, looked up.

To grow till it trips him, he had chuckled. To grow and grow till the horsehair chair is stuffed full and the sofa's plump to squeaking. The dark man will come, driving like Jehu down Dedman Creek hill, bags open, and you'll sell him manes and tails enough to buy the muskrat coat she's wanting.

That's natural, Bill had said. It's natural to sell them to the dealer. But it's not natural to pluck them out one by one – to pull them out in the vanity of riding round the country like a heathen. Why for did God give a horse a tail? To flick the flies offen his flank.

Stella had been told that no one wielded a gelder's knife more skilfully than Bill. It was not unnatural since he had been raised to the trade. Every year the spring calves were rounded up and corralled in the enclosure near the alkali lakes. It was not natural to raise a herd of bulls. Steers were the natural herd for a man to keep – plump, sleek steers.

Swift's buyer – thought Stella, remembering Williams – running his hand over the well-rounded flank, watching the scales tip, choosing this, rejecting that, would cry in admiration, well done, faithful servant, accept the dollars prepared for you and depart to Deep Hollow Creek, for your herd is better than that of your brother.

Stella looked back at the bulls. They had abandoned the bank and were making abortive dashes at one another, throwing up dirt with their feet.

Out of a clump of pine trees a low mist drifted. Stella shivered. She remembered what Farish had told Miriam about Annunciata's baby.

The mist is death, he said. When they see the mist creeping on the ground they hide from it.

Along the ground the mist drifted. It curled erect and

blossomed in a crown of gentians – blue against the shadow of the hill.

Then she heard an undulating voice crying, Throw off the bands of custom, break down the barriers. Nature stirs deep within you. I am the primitive urge, out of the blastoderm endlessly calling.

There to the left was a pile of stones, heaped from the last great road clearing. Slowly they manoeuvred into place, each a face – face rolling on face – each face a wheel, each wheel a face. Then from the cairn came a voice – thin, precise, dry –

Taurus, tauri.

And a stone rolling from the pile echoed –

Lapis, lapidis.

And the mist rose higher and the gentians burned from blue to the red of Indian paint-brush –

Flamen, flaminis.

And out of the bosom of the hill came a soft groan –

Man, man.

Pigeon accelerated his pace without external stimulus. Darkness was flattening out the roundness of the hills. High up, bark echoed bark as a pair of coyotes crossed the ridge.

Life would go on. The fool-hens were nesting. The grass was lengthening on the hills, and the bulls wandering in the road, pricked on by nature, would return to their cows. Nature was unfolding inevitably. Things gestated and dropped to destruction soon or late.

Mockett would shoulder his spade after he had turned out the cow, would pile earth here, level it there, letting the water through this channel, stopping its flow in that. He would tap on the door, Stella knew, and leave a lettuce and some radishes, or the thinnings of the carrots. And Mamie, peering from behind the veil of lace in the public parlour, would say, The old fool has no sense – giving what it's natural to sell. Then Bill would clap an extra ten on the next pound of coffee he sold to Antoine Billy over the counter, since Antoine Billy could not calculate the market price and the cent and a half per mile cartage, and the extra bonus for manna in the wilderness.

After Mockett had done his chores – after he had thinned the carrots or sown a second growth of lettuce – he would do his turn across the counter. Putting the mail into sacks, sorting it into piles, he would meditate on a life which came mirrored in the pages of the *Manchester Guardian*.

Only once he had complained to Stella in a moment of imperative confidence.

All these years, he had said, since I knew what life was and an education – since I got them their school here – since I've been the pin in the link between them and the government in Victoria – ever since I was a draper's apprentice in Manchester I've been despised and contemned and used to the end of vanity.

Do you see this? he said, flattening the paper out on the counter – the Japanese in Manchuria – trouble in Spain – the market falling, falling. It's not natural, he said, to play at God Almighty in this narrow rocky pit.

ELEVEN

Beside the bench stood two buckets. When Stella woke the next morning after her slow progress from the Porcupine she remembered that one was quite empty. From the other she filled the kettle. Lilac had gone to the Rock.

This afternoon – Stella thought, looking at the saddle which she had dropped the night before, looking at the peg on which she should have hung it – I will walk to the reserve to see if Antoine Billy's Christine can come down for a few days to help. Had Lilac been in the valley Stella would have sent for her – that is, she would have gone to get her. She had come one day a week after Miriam had left the cabin for the Porcupine – on foot through the snow. She had brought buckets of water from the creek. She had washed, taking the galvanized tub from the nail, putting it on a bench, warming the coal-oil tins on the stove. She had scrubbed the floor boards while cold creeping under the door had left an ice fringe before the water dried. The steam from the washing had iced the panes of glass inside so that the light came dully strained through a triple thickness. She had taken the clothes, stiff from the line, and thawed them on a rack by the stove.

Mamie had murmured, had whispered that no one should get a whole day's pay for a half-day's work.

There can be very little to do in that small cabin, she had said. Lilac won't want to work for other people.

Stella remembered her comment now. She turned to speak to Juno but she had let her out with the pups. They were lying in the earth – which she had softened round the rhubarb plants – sprawling in the soft earth, casually aloof.

Recalled from she knew not when the whispered reproach brought with it remembered resentment.

There is not much fear of that, Mamie. In the store, over the counter, Mockett weighs your tea and your sugar and your flour.

Mockett weighing sweat in the balance.

– Your wages, Lilac. A quart of coal-oil which you don't need, my dear. God gives a light which lights every man, squaw, and papoose in the narrow valley of life. The night is long – and for sleeping.

– Flour, Lilac – cold and damp, and yellow as the oats in stook.

– Crying in the night with the belly-ache, was she – crying in the night?

– Your man wants nails to shoe his horse as ranchmen do?

– He's picked up a shoe cast by Bill's mare – pounded it, fitting a splay foot into a vice of iron?

– A horse has four feet, my dear.

– Lord keep her hands from picking and stealing.

Mockett's voice, lifting the curtain for the interlude.

Over by the stove Sam sits waiting for the stage to come with his order from Simpsons – his order from Eaton's. Since Mockett, the coyote, underbid him in the mail contract he sits waiting for Bill's boy, Clarence, to haul in the packages.

One and a half cents a pound. Not if they come by His Majesty's mail – straight from Simpsons, straight from Eaton's – addressed in letters big enough for the old dog to read without reaching for his spectacles, without hefting the package and mauling it and shaking it. There is no bill of lading, old fox. It came by His Majesty's mail, only a name on the thick brown cover – city efficiency, city efficiency. My parcel, sir. No need to shake and listen – to listen and shake.

Lilac had gone to the Rock – she and her man in the wagon, dogs behind the wheels, dogs under the switching tail of the horse, daring his feet, lolling behind, indifferent. They would pick up the children at the mission school on the way down.

Between them on the high spring seat sat Angela, legs dangling. This year, next year, some time, never. If she lived she too would go   packed off some autumn day with the other children and Lilac would know a new loneliness. No more rising in the night to comfort a voice crying.

Write, she had said – Stella remembered – write to Eaton's for good white flour. Send my money for the work. It's the belly-ache – crying in the night – crying with the belly-ache.

Christine might come.

It was only a half-hour's walk to the reservation. In the afternoon Stella went.

There the valley opened a little. From the edge of the creek rose a thin shaft of smoke, bending and flattening over the rite of purification – Johnny in the steam bath, flat stones smoking.

It was an awful shock, Mamie had said, the first time I saw him. I'll never get used to such things. He was wrinkled and naked like a newborn rat, standing in the sunshine by the creek for decent people to see as they passed. I don't go that way now, she said, I stay here or go in the car. There are things

Bill says no decent woman should see and Johnny's one of them – just like a rat – naked and wrinkled like the newborn rats Mockett found in the nest under the counter.

Sunshine soaked the tops of the hills. It had seeped down fibre by fibre into the valley. Now it was drying up. Close by the caves a coyote sat on a ledge. Something living moved across the pool of light – left by some delusive refraction – trapped like a pool in the valley from the ebbing flood of light.

Outside the log cabin sat Antoine Billy. The clay chinking was crumbling between the logs, spilling away the life of the house over the rough surface of the logs – falling back, grain by grain, to the earth from which it had been pilfered. Antoine Billy sat breathing life and warmth and rest from the quietness.

He was wearing one of Mockett's dollar-fifty shirts – red crossed on blue, blue latticed on red, a week's wages in the field.

Joseph's coats – Mockett had said, resting his pipe loosely in the cavity between his yellow teeth – that's how they like them and that's how I stock them. Polka dots for the girls, plaid for the boys. There's no end to the work you can get out of them for a plaid shirt.

Up on the shelf in piles – with the bolts and the nails, with the kerosene and the flour, with the tins of sardines, the bottles of pain-killer and Sloan's liniment – he put the shirts.

How does one speak to a man sitting wrapped in the silence of a spring day – sitting wrapped in the majesty of a plaid shirt on his own doorstep, Stella thought.

Perhaps Christine would come out. Perhaps Johnny, having sweated away the scum of winter, would crack the twigs as he came from the creek bottom.

The coyote sat silent on the ledge like a shadow on the rock. Only the practised eye could see the substance in the shadow.

Farish had told her.

Coyote the god – the great god Coyote, coming in the night – coming in the hunting season – tumbling men off ledges and women in their beds – lighting his torch of bulrush at the household fire – unstoppering the corroding liniment of midnight flame – playing his tricks so that only the dark shadows spied him – dipping into other men's buckets – spitting in the lake until he made it green with his poison, salt forming round the edge where the cattle drank – flesh drying on the bone which he had touched – babies dying in their baskets – the whole world turned to a Sodom of salt.

Antoine? she called. Antoine. He stirred – skin twitched, muscles tightened.

Antoine?

Yass.

He straightened.

It's a fine mild evening.

Yass.

You've been having a little sleep?

N-o.

I wonder if Christine could come down for a day or two? Stella asked. I've cracked a rib and Lilac's gone to the Rock. There's some washing to do and water to get – and a little wood.

Yass, he said, ask him.

In he went, slipping round the corner of the door, pulling the door close against curious glances.

———

The clock ticked in the House, marking the hours, the days, the years. Down in the book went the days. Over the counter Mockett handed the flour and the shirts. The seasons came and went – sometimes too soon, sometimes too late. Man slipped into the sun's embrace and out of it and lit coal-oil lamps to cheat the darkness.

Antoine Billy came out.

N-o, he said.

Then with unwonted expansiveness he went on, smiling a little with the side of his mouth, as if slipping a pipe into the hollow between the teeth.

I would like him to go for you.

His hands spread out as if he were flattening a paper, as if he rested them on the edge of the counter.

My woman say n-o. I would like very much – but I n-o can make him work. Next month perhaps I come myself to chop wood for you.

Stella walked home. Only the mind endlessly questioned. Seared on the retina – or by it, or through it – seared on the flat disc guarded by memory.

No, no, she didn't want to see it – a man on a horse raising a whip, letting the great bull tongue of it lick and fleer and sear the flesh of an old greybeard in the street – the mayor in all his pomp of tweed and hair lotion and shaving lotion and devotion standing on the cenotaph reading the riot act – men rifling the counters – men hurling bricks through windows – men sitting in the sun – sitting in the post office waiting for the mail from nowhere – tear bombs and jeer bombs.

Only hate and fear, she thought, the hand on the counter

reaching for the pain-killer – the pyrethrum – the hobble – the halter – the chin-strap – the check-rein.

What is that noise? she recited to herself softly. The wind under the door.

What is that noise now? What is the wind doing?

Nothing again nothing.

The next day, when Elizabeth came to bring some moccasins she had made, Stella asked her if she would come to work for a few days. Elizabeth said nothing. She was intent on the deal. Her method of exchange she had learned from Mockett and from nature itself.

To those who gave, nature made return – a deer for a bullet, spuds for the planting and digging. Sometimes a grouse winged by another fell on the doorstep. Then one gave thanks to Coyote as one gave thanks if Mockett passed a sweet across the counter to a reaching hand, slipping on the stained wood, nail following the groove back and forth – while those who had, bartered.

A leetle bit of tea, she said, a leetle bit of oil – a leetle bit of flour.

The goods were laid on the table.

A leetle bit of thread.

No – with a shake of the head – theek thread.

So.

And thirty-five cents.

The deal was complete.

With the money, thought Stella, she is in possession of an undetermined joy. It is power over Mockett.

Why hadn't she asked for more, she wondered.

Forty-five cents, she suggested, prying to know, indifferently curious.

Elizabeth's eyes turned full on her. One hand reached out for the moccasins. The other arm circled the flour, the oil, the thread.

Thirty-five cents, she insisted.

What do you want to get? Stella asked.

Thirty-five cents, she intoned again.

Stella counted the money out on the table – a quarter and a dime.

She shook her head. Three dimes and a nickel.

She caught them up.

Perhaps, Stella suggested, you could come for a day or two to help me.

Yass, she said.

Then I'll see you in the morning, Stella suggested.

Y-ass.

The curtains were pulled. The lamp was lighted. The stage had brought letters, a newspaper, a package of books, Gide, *Siegfried et la Limousin*, *Europa*, *The New Statesman*, the old copy of the *Religio* she had asked for, falling open at its usual place:

I could never divide myself from any man on the difference of an opinion, or be angry with his judgment for not agreeing with me in that from which perhaps within a few days I should dissent myself. Every man is not a proper champion for truth. . . .

The pups were asleep on their rug. Juno sat by her chair.

There is always a jest, she said, putting the book down open on the table. Juno and the Paycock – there you sit, your glory and your woe asleep behind you on the mat; here I sit, asking What are the stars, what is the moon.

There was a tap on the door – a tap between loud and soft, a tap between a demand and a request. As she opened the door she heard a horse breathing. She smelled sweat and leather.

A lamp burning up oil, she thought, a lamp throwing off black fumes – a human body . . .

She reached for the flashlight.

Come in, she said.

He stood there holding his hat, his spurs dragging on the floor. She did not know him.

There is a courage born of caste, of position, of prerogative. No one would dare to hurt me, she thought.

Juno stood over the pups, rigid.

Yes? she questioned.

Leezbeeth, he said, I come to tell you Leezbeeth n-o come. I come to tell you I n-o let Leezbeeth come. I come to tell you Leezbeeth n-o work for other people. My woman n-o work for n-o-one.

TWELVE

On the hills the wild strawberries ripened.

Every year, Mamie said, they bring me a pailful for jam. There is nothing else in the world like wild strawberry jam.

They pick them for me, she said. They are so small and so hard to find that it takes hours to pick a pailful.

The Farishes had gone and the grass grew up in the field at the Porcupine.

I'll have to turn something in there, said Bill. It's a nuisance to have feed up there when they need it but a man might as well get all that's to be got.

What they wanted I don't know, Rose said, speaking of the Farishes to Stella, who sat at the end of the kitchen table watching her shape dough into loaves. What they wanted here I don't know.

I suppose down at the House she's up for the summer, she said, up for the agent when he comes to play games and to see about the flume – up and about others' business.

I went – she said, looking across the loaves – after a

chicken and I saw the land across the river stretching green along Boulder Creek. But the hills, she said, the hills are naked and brown as an egg.

She wiped the flour from her hands on the sides of her dress.

Since you were coming to tea I made a crumble cake, she said, shoving aside the cotton curtain which covered the pantry door.

I'll fill the teapot, she said.

Sam came in to tea. He sat at the other end of the kitchen table. Stella looked at the grey curls, damp above his thin face.

What are you going to do with your livestock, he asked, when it's closed up?

He jerked his head towards the schoolhouse.

I don't know, she said, I really don't know.

I'll take the palomino back, he said, any time you say — and keep him till you come again.

Rose looked up and the light from the window fell across her eyes.

Not even Mr. Thompson came back, she said.

The funniest thing I ever heard tell in this country, said Sam with apparent irrelevance, was what Hawkins' pardner told me. He said Clintock called his fee-pup Selassie. It's not a name at all, he said. Why next to Juno it's the most ridiculous name I ever heard clapped on a dog in all the time my ears has been listening to the names of brute beasts.

The old lady can rest quiet at home since the Porcupine's empty, he went on, and there will be others will rest quieter too.

He picked his cup up with both hands and tipped it until the surface of the tea slanted to the rim, mirroring his thin face and grey hair.

It's not such a bad idea, he said, having a mug of tea before milking the cow. It gives a man a chance to take the weight off his feet.

Everywhere the life which had quickened was passing through time to fulfilment and still new life quickened. The cotton-woods leafed green, and in the afternoon light the stems showed white against the hill.

Every day Stella rode Pigeon up and across the flats above the creek – over the rolling grass range where the cows grazed with calves beside them.

One day she saw two stallions fighting, reared up by the edge of an alkali lake, the mares crowded together round a curve of the rolling earth. Pigeon whinnied with fear.

Another day, dropping the lines, she watched a blue grouse courting, the hen dancing under a dock leaf while the cock drummed his desire.

It's Mamie, she thought, teaching Bill the hesitation waltz.

Everywhere the thing which wasn't, became, and the thing which was, altered.

Like the other inhabitants of the creek and like the bears which slept in winter, she had lost weight and the trousers which had constricted her knees in the cold weeks before Christmas were furled and secured with a rawhide boot-lace bought from Mockett at the store.

That there was no rawhide stay for the mind was a fact that she had come to accept. The mind took care of itself – growing and expanding from some inner force. It could be destroyed from without as the leaf could be destroyed by the restless hand. It could not be made with the hand, though, as a cabin is made or a skyscraper. And if it could fall prey to chance and nameless accident it withered as it grew by some principle inherent in itself.

Old Gabrielle, scenting the approach of her departure, had come to the cabin. She sat fingering a pile of *New Statesman*s that she had asked for to make kindling. Her eye had been caught by the pile under the table and she had asked for them as if they were the business which had brought her.

She sat and smoked in silence.

M'bee you got teapot f'm-e, she said, eyeing the shelf.

You can have it when I go, Stella said. Come back then.

M'bee swoter, Gabrielle went on.

Stella had given Lilac a box of sweaters for the children. They were the bright-coloured sweaters which she had worn under her dark suits. The alkali water had shrunk them to child's size.

She looked at Gabrielle. No doubt she was cold most of the time. She went to the trunk in the bedroom and got out a black shawl-collared sweater which had at one time been part of her school uniform. It was still thick and warm and the breaks in the thread had been mended.

I won't need it again, she thought, not when I go from here.

Gabrielle sat with it in her hand for a moment. Then she put it on the bench beside her.

N-o, she said.

Then again, N-o. Why, she said, pushing it further from her, I got better than him myse'f.

Then she gathered up the papers and went.

Lilac's Angela in crimson – Gabrielle in the aunt's knitted suit – Aloyisha a green-lace butterfly in the sunlight, Stella thought.

Perhaps it is as well that she didn't take it, she said to Juno. I might have seen her in it and by some strange delusion fancied her as myself.

In the evening Juno sat as she usually did by the table.

When Stella finished supper she poured the coffee. She reached for the matches to light her cigarette. She lit the cigarette absently then, bending, offered the light to Juno.

When the match burned her finger she became a spectator of the scene – Juno by the chair – herself – Browne open at her elbow – the match extended – the twinge of seared flesh.

I don't know, she said to Juno, I really don't know who is mad. It is time for us to get out of here, she said. Juno sat.

I'll try to find something for Gabrielle, she thought. She can get it when she comes for the teapot.

AFTERWORD

BY JANE URQUHART

F ew of us who went on to be writers (and, I expect, many of us who did not) will ever forget our first encounter with Sheila Watson's visionary and poetic novel *The Double Hook*, an encounter that often took place in an undergraduate course in Canadian literature. For some of us, it was an electrifying awakening – one poet I know says she felt, while reading, that she was sitting stark naked in a field filled with lightning. For some of us, entering the text became identified as the moment when we first understood the power of spare, tough language. Whatever the case, coming to know *The Double Hook* furnished many young writers with a sense of liberation, the notion that, even in a country as uncertain and as conservative as Canada then was, we were no longer required, necessarily, to play by the old, safe rules. The book gave us a kind of permission to reach out beyond ourselves and rein in the light, or to dig deep into our inner selves and pull out the darkness. We felt free to take language apart and put it back together again. And, perhaps most important, a veil that had existed between ourselves and our own landscape was lifted forever. *The Double Hook* made

it possible for us to recognize and to explore the deeply arche-
typal qualities of our own place, our own existence. *The Double
Hook* gave us confidence in metaphor.

How odd, then, in 1992, so many years later, to be pre-
sented with *Deep Hollow Creek*, the novel Watson wrote as a
young woman in the 1930s, after she had spent two years teaching in the Cariboo country at Dog Creek – the very ground her
imagination would return to when writing *The Double Hook*
more than a decade later. Every writer brings a new self to each
book. Perhaps, in the best of all possible worlds, each author
would have the patience to wait a full seven years, long enough
for every cell in the human body to replace itself, before
approaching another manuscript. In Watson's case, it appears
that, although she would have necessarily brought a new
writer-self to *The Double Hook*, we were to learn by reading
Deep Hollow Creek that her inner geography had remained the
same. Something about the harshness, the tough beauty of the
Cariboo country had clearly penetrated deep into her uncon-
scious, so much so that it became the primary theatre in which
her imagination would want to act out its dramas.

Watson went to the remote Cariboo country in 1934
because it was the only place that had agreed to hire her as a
teacher. "I didn't choose," she remarked, "it chose me." And it
seems to me that this rugged terrain chose her as a writer as
well as a teacher, chose her, entered her, and claimed her to such
an extent that, regardless of passing time or physical distance,
it would continue to haunt her and demand a response from
her. Years later, for instance, long after she had finished the
manuscript of the book you now hold in your hands, the landscape of the Cariboo and Dog Creek would return to her mind
as she stood at one of Toronto's busiest intersections, tap her on
the shoulder if you like, and insist that she write *The Double*

Hook. Like Emily Brontë, Watson was given instruments of stone and earth, sky and weather to work with, and again like Brontë, she was able to build something universal and enduring with these most basic and powerful of tools.

For all its similarities of landscape and, to a certain extent, of character, *Deep Hollow Creek* is, however, a very different book from *The Double Hook.* To my mind, while *The Double Hook* is a book about profound wisdom and knowledge, *Deep Hollow Creek* speaks to us, through the thoughts of its main character, Stella, of exploration and discovery. A young woman highly educated in things of an intellectual nature, Stella has come into the valley in order to make contact with the sort of physical existence that does not depend on, nor, for that matter, have time for cerebral reflection and scientific analysis. Which is not to say that she herself intends to give up such things – reference is made on the second page to the box of books she has brought with her – but she is consciously, and respectfully, paying attention to the life of toil and endurance that is being enacted all around her. When she observes, near the beginning of the book, that the bitter bread baked by the farm wife, Rose, is a "peculiar emblem," she does so with interest and compassion, not with malice, just as she silently wonders about her own educated view:

> Through Sassetta's eyes or Edmund Spenser's I see in the shadow of Limbo the red cross – and they see it because the light glances off and reflects from the fire which warms their shoulders as they work. I have always taken the compass as a thing to be held. Yet the hand falters measuring the fleeting body of flame.

These opening pages, then, present us with what I believe is a central theme in the book, refined culture thrown into the midst of stark nature and, with the marriage of these opposites, the birth of narrative.

Stella becomes a person to whom a tale is told, Coleridge's wedding guest or Emily Brontë's Joseph Lockwood, mere moments after she enters the territory of the valley. One by one the inhabitants tell her their stories:

> Always the story came. The variations were only those inspired by the moment. The story was a part of the fabric of their lives.

Mamie Flower tells her the story of Rose Flower and vice versa. Sam Flower tells her how she came to board with his family and makes a fleet and fascinating reference to the importation of camels into the vicinity. Nicholas Farish brings rumours, predictions, and news of the native peoples, and Sam tells the tragic story of Williams's failure and suicide. Mockett, the store owner, politician, and school trustee, keeps tabs on the outside world by reading the *Manchester Guardian*. Each report is delivered to Stella, and through Stella to us, with a startling lack of sentimentality and embellishment, which, remarkably enough, permits the pure poetry and drama of the event to become clear. After Sam has recounted the sad history of Williams's demise, for example, his boy George remarks:

> A dead body's an awful thing in this country now. . . . Summer the ground's baked hard as nails. Winters she's froze. When old McIntosh died they had to put him in a tree out of the coyotes' way until the ground

thawed in the spring. Heat and cold between them gets
the best of things.

In each tale there is a grim acceptance of huge elemental
forces, of "the bleak view of brown earth across the river," and
of the smallness of human concerns in comparison. In a world
such as this, we quickly come to understand, there is abso-
lutely no room for vanity.

About halfway through the book Stella moves into her
own cabin and starts to live completely in the landscape where
she has found herself. She acquires a horse and a dog who
become, in this sparsely populated terrain, central characters,
each with a will of his or her own. She becomes engrossed
with the physical details of the perceived world: ice on
windows, a white enamelled hand basin, "the brittle scraping
of the frozen bush branches against the logs outside." A friend
named Miriam, a sort of alter ego, joins Stella in the house,
and both young women make contact with the native people
in the area. Stella comes to accept the spiritual nature of the
landscape as it is manifested by Coyote, the trickster god of
the Shuswap people – his magic, his elusiveness, how "only
the practiced eye could see the substance in the shadow." She
also comes to understand the dignity and pride of the native
people. When she attempts to hire a native girl to help her
after breaking a rib as the result of a fall from her horse, she
is met with resistance. "My woman," a young man tells her,
"n-o work for n-o-one."

Eventually, like the light of understanding, spring bursts
from the side of a hill in the form of the water released from
the winter's ice. The combination of this compelling symbol
and Stella's fear that she might miss "the moment of resurrection," that she "might sit reading while the fountain gushed

from the frozen bones of the hill," reveals the importance of the spiritual journey she has taken since she came into the valley. As always, Watson's imagist's eye, her ability to recognize in the outer world a mirror of the inner life of her character, is as extraordinary as her timing is perfect. When Stella says to herself, and to her dog Juno, that had she never come to Deep Hollow Creek, she would never "have seen through the shroud of printers' ink, through to the embalmed essence," and that "the word is a flame burning in a dark glass," we know exactly what she means. She has shoved aside the freight of her intellect, put away the compass and its measurements, and looked directly into the flame of life itself.

And Stella has not flinched in the face of the dark glass surrounding life, surrounding "the word," the beginning of all things. But then Watson never shrank from darkness. She seemed to know instinctively, and from the beginning, that just as the stars need enough dark to shine, a work of literature is incomplete if it does not disclose the darkness as well as the light. "When you fish for the glory," she states in *The Double Hook*, "you catch the darkness too." There are always lighter moments, dogs named after rivers, a regional version of Macbeth's witches in a school play, Mamie teaching Bill the "hesitation waltz," redemption coming in the form of a fountain of water tumbling over boulders, or sunshine soaking the tops of these hills and seeping "fibre by fibre into the valley." But there is also always "the great god Coyote, coming in the night – coming in the hunting season – tumbling men off ledges and women in their beds – lighting his torch of bulrush at the household fire –"

BY SHEILA WATSON